November 12, 2011.

To/Alex,
Very Best,
Andrew McIntyre.

The Short, the Long, and the Tall

by
Andrew McIntyre

MERILANG PRESS
Bodyfuddau
Trawsfynydd
Gwynedd LL41 4UW
Wales
United Kingdom

First Edition

A CIP catalogue record for this book is available
from the British Library

ISBN: 978-0-9555430-7-4

Dedicated to:

Daffni Percival and David Gardiner for their vital help and guidance, thereby making this book possible.

Deborah Clearwaters for hours of formatting, endless patience, and unconditional love and support.

My Mother and Fumiko Hasegawa, who saved me from destitution in the 1990s. Fumiko Hasegawa for 30 years of love, friendship, and wisdom.

Marlow.

Table of Contents

Introduction

I was captivated by the writing process from an early age, when I boarded at the Downs School, Colwall, about 40 years ago. Influenced by W.H. Auden's tenure there as a teacher in the 1930s, the Oxford educated English masters passionately encouraged creative writing. Auden's legacy was The Badger, the school's magazine, and there was intense competition to be published. I left the Downs, embarking on the traditional English middle class path towards a practical career. Composing a story became an increasingly distant happy childhood memory in a process of studied indoctrination, where Art was portrayed as impractical and decadent, something you needed to shun if you wanted to progress in the world.

Two decades later, amid appalling personal circumstances, I began to write as a means of survival, to focus my mind during long sleepless winter nights. About ten years ago, with my situation more stable, I started submitting work to magazines for publication. These stories emerged partly from a need to find creation beyond the inane repetition of daily existence. They have also functioned as a catharsis for my frustration with the challenges of this troubled decade, difficulties which will remain. One of the essences of Art is surely to provide a catalyst for recognition, potential solution, and progress. I hope I can meet the reader in this ethereal place.

Art for Art's Sake,
Money for God's Sake

VE Day, 1945. I think it was Jimmy's idea to go to Maxim's. We were in Paris, we were Americans, we'd liberated Europe. Victory was ours. C'mon, let's go live it up, he said, We deserve it. So we went, twelve of us. We'd all been in the front line at some point covering stories, we were alive, we needed to celebrate. There was a rumor Hemingway might show. I was pretty new so I just followed, I was very keen to meet Hemingway. The rest of them were a bunch of hacks I didn't recognize, and a couple of art critics.

So we were getting into the meal, everyone talking at once. I started with escargots, then roast duck. The bottles kept coming. Soon we were all drunk, and people started telling jokes. Hey listen to this one, yelled Jimmy, Which artist has dirty fingers? Why don't you shut it, someone yelled back, You've got a big mouth Jimbo. Everyone jocular, no malice. No seriously, slurred Jimmy, Which artist has dirty fingers? No-one was listening, so Jimmy stood up and yelled, Picasso. There was a moment's silence, then we were on the floor, like it was the funniest thing we'd ever heard.

The meal went on like this for about three hours, by which time everyone had put away at least two bottles of wine. We were toasting dead colleagues, singing songs. A couple of guys had fallen asleep. I was sitting back nursing a glass of cognac smoking a big Havana thinking of the good life, the war over, and we could go home. New era, new world. It was hard to believe.

Someone called for the check. The head waiter arrived, very correct, very respectful. We thanked him. Someone hollered, Vive La France and started singing the Marseillaise, the only one amongst us who knew any proper French, aside from asking for wine or a girl. The check did the rounds, no-one seemed anxious to pull out their wallet. When Jimmy saw it his eyes nearly popped out of his head. He handed it to me without a word. I did the math, recounted, repeated the process, checked the conversion, allowed for zeros. No mistake. $600. More than my life savings. I didn't even have two bucks on me. I'm cleaned out, whispered Jimmy. It turned out we had twenty bucks between us. Everyone thought someone else was going to pay, or else it was on the house because we were Americans and we'd won the war.

When the head waiter found out, he was no longer respectful and correct. An argument ensued, negotiations about washing up all night, calling the police. A couple of waiters entered the fray. Things were getting nasty. Then to cap it all one of the waiters made a remark about how this would never have happened when the Germans were there, the Germans always paid on the spot, they behaved better than the Americans. A scuffle started, one of the guys took a swing at the waiter who swung back, other guys trying to break it up, getting into a mix up themselves. Some military police arrived accompanied by two plainclothes officers. Things settled down, everyone straightening their jackets and ties, while we parlayed what to do.

I saw a stocky little guy with dark hair talking to the head waiter. I'd vaguely noticed him, and the broad he was with, no-one else paid them any attention, but they'd been watching us. They were at a table in the far corner, the woman dark and very beautiful like a gypsy. The head waiter listened, nodding, and he gave the little guy a menu. The little guy scribbled something on the card and returned it to the head waiter. The head waiter studied it, then he strolled over to our table, a big smile on his face. Gentlemen, he enunciated, The bill is taken care of, you may now leave. Knowing your predicament, Pablo Picasso has produced a drawing for Maxim's in lieu of your payment. He wishes you his warmest compliments. In the subsequent chaos, I looked at the drawing briefly before it was whisked away. First I saw eyebrows and a nose, but when I looked a second time I perceived a pair of buttocks and a pen.

Dirty War

War's been going on a long time now. How long? Sometimes I can't remember. Three years. Five years. Twenty years. No-one seems to know when it started. You ask around and everyone's got a different idea of when it began. Maybe it's been going on forever. We don't talk about it anymore. Johnny and me that is. Johnny Scotland.

We kicked them out of Kabul. That was the easy part. We had them surrounded in the end, carpet bombed them, annihilated them, there was nothing left. Then we moved into Kabul. That's it, we all thought, It's over. They're gone. For a few days there was a party. We clean the city, get a garrison going, clean uniforms, airlifts, medical supplies, the whole bureaucracy of victory. The general makes an inspection, the journalists drink their scotch in the afternoon. Then one morning, we're sitting down to breakfast and KABOOOOM KABOOOOM KABOOOOM we're cowering under the table. I thought it was exercises but it was too damn close, and then a building explodes across the street. The war had started again before it had even ended. But who's shooting?

When we find out what's going on no-one can believe it. The guys we had surrounded, the guys we annihilated, now they've got us surrounded. All the roles reversed. We besieged them now they're besieging us. Act Two. Kabul's ringed by mountains you see. Control the mountains and you control the city. Infantry 101. The high ground. Remember the song, Take the high ground and hold it . . . Who the hell ever decided to build the capital in such a crummy location? Ought to be put up against a wall and shot. Sarajevo the same, I was there too a while back. Fat cities stuck in a valley. Makes no sense. But the capital's the capital, and it's gotta be controlled. That's all there is to it. So here we are and here we will remain because at the moment all the roads are held by the rebels and there's no way out or in. All our supplies come from the air. We're Up the Khyber, as the Brits used to say except no-one wants to remember what happened to them back in the 1840s. Maybe we'll have to walk to Jalalabad in the middle of winter.

So it's the same old thing. We bomb them, they bomb us, they show pictures of dead children to the newspapers, we do the same, they grab some of our boys, we grab some of theirs. We torture each other trying to break through, but nothing is happening. It goes on and on, no end in sight, no solution forthcoming. I work for the STD, Special Tactics Department that is. Getting guys in, getting them out. We take prisoners and then we try to break them so they'll tell us their positions. Problem is we often wind up killing them before they tell us anything. Hard boys these fundamentalists. Mental, and no fun. There's just so much the human body can take. Usually they die. The only thing they've ever told us over and over is God is Great. You've gotta admire them. The harder we hit them the harder they fight, the harder they get, like tempered steel. We've done everything. Dental stuff, no man can take. Electrics all over the body. I've hammered toes flat with a sledge, hung weights from their balls, used piano wire, torn out fingernails, toenails, tongues, you name it. I've shoved tubes down their dicks, tubes up their butts, poked out eyes, blown away knees with a small caliber weapon. Most of it useless. No results and it goes on for a long time. Inevitably they wind up dying, shock, loss of blood. And there's nothing we can do. There's just so much we know. I'm limited by my education, after all. Torture is open to research just like any other discipline.

So one day I'm sitting in The Room, with Johnny Scotland, having a coffee break because we've been working on one of these boys for two days and he's about to go. A big bearded thug, muscled like a Bulgar. We haven't gained an iota of information. We've tried the usual and he just spits blood at us when he gets a chance and yells incomprehensible oaths that the translator can't follow, and I've hit him so hard out of sheer frustration that my fist has started to swell. The whole fucking thing's absurd, and we're just going through the motions. Gotta write something in the log book, We did this, we did that etc. but information was not forthcoming. End of story. Tomorrow he'll be thrown into the incinerator just like the last two hundred and seventy three, although Johnny swears we've already made three hundred.

Hard case, I say. Yeah, says Johnny, What's new? We smoke our cigarettes in silence. Your fist's swelling, he adds. Looks that way, I say taking a drag. Johnny Scotland. We joined together long ago. Marines, Special Operations. We went to Granada, Panama, Lebanon, me and Johnny. We saw the end of Nam. Then they moved us up into the STD. We've had all kinds of guys go through The Room. The best were the Serbs. I like people to look the part. The motherfucking Serbs. These boys looked big and tough. They were big and tough, when they were shelling schoolgirls in Sarajevo from the comfort of the hills, or gunning down families in Kosovo. Big tough boys with shaven heads and lots of muscles. But give them to me and Johnny and we had them squealing for their mothers. Like stuck pigs. It was good to see, a job with a meaning. Seeing big muscled Serbs weeping and begging for mercy. After a couple of days in The Room they told us everything we wanted to know. Clipping off a Serb toe with wire cutters. Those big fucking faggot rapists. I used to look forward to it.

And Johnny Scotland. Hey, he's a funny guy. I love it when someone asks his name and he replies, Scotland, John Scotland, and the stupid fuck who's asked him grins and says, Your folks from Scotland? Me too. And Johnny just stares the guy down and says, My folks are not from Scotland you stupid fuck, they're Swedish, Swedes, and he goes into this long aggravated monologue about how his name comes from the Swedish Schøttlund or Schüttlund or some such crap and how Schöttlund is a remote island off the Swedish Arctic where the Schötts lived, and the Schötts were a fierce tribe of proto-Vikings who invented violence, and apparently they ate the brains of their enemies. None of this is documented in conventional Swedish history, but Johnny says it's true, and he says it's just because the Swedes have turned into sappy peaceniks that they don't want this part of their history documented. And someone in the STD once pointed out that Jeffrey Dahmer was of good

Scandinavian stock and look at what he was capable of, and Johnny agreed, Yes he probably was a descendent of the Schötts, and maybe the Dharma was the way to be. And it's unwise to argue with Johnny. I once saw him bite a guy's nose off when we were on leave in Miami (the guy was bothering Johnny when he was trying to relax in a bar), and Johnny didn't spit the nose out like most guys would have done. No sir, he swallowed it without even chewing it. Johnny Scotland. I've never stopped liking the taste of boogers, he said afterwards, when we were walking out of the bar. I've often wondered what Johnny talks about at his high school reunions.

So Johnny looks at me and grins. What's bothering you? I ask. Hey, a joke, says Johnny, A joke. Let's try something new, see what happens. Something new? I say irritated. Yeah, he replies, Listen. I've been thinking. Have you ever thought? Why these guys are so fucking mad. The Israelis, the mujahadeen. Not really, I say, That's just the way they are isn't it. I mean what else are they going to do? Exactly, says Johnny, Exactly. I mean listen to this, I was thinking. The Muslims, the Jews, they're the same damn thing right, speak the same language almost, they're all Semites, they're the same fucking race for chrissake. So why the fuck are they always trying to kill each other? If they're the same I mean.

I ponder this piece of logic for a couple of moments before saying, Maybe it's because they are the same that they hate each other. I mean if I had to live with me all the time I'd wind up killing myself. Johnny sprays coffee everywhere laughing, On the button my dear Watson, on the button, that's exactly it. Think about it. The whole of their life they don't get any girls, they don't even see girls. All they see, if they're lucky, is a walking blanket. That ain't a fucking girl. Unless you're into jacking off over blankets. Ever see girls knocking about the streets of Karachi when you were there? Or Jeddah? Remember? There are no fucking girls. Same for our Orthodox Jewish friends. All the women are inside. At the best of times, when they've really got their rocks off, most of these guys have just fucked boys up the butt, and that's no way to live by any stretch of the imagination. So what's your point? I ask, Where are you trying to get to with all this academic analysis? Johnny grins, taking a drag on his cigarette. That's why they're all so mad, he explains, smoke pouring out of his mouth, Why they're so pissed at one another, why they're pissed with everything and everyone. They never get any cunt. No cunt ever. And they're all circumcised to boot. What a combination. You'd be pissed. Think about it. A man who can't get any cunt is inevitably going to be seriously pissed, give him a gun, and instead of cunt he fills his head with religion, you've got a problem. These guys would do anything to get into the pants of some blonde walking the streets of LA. They see us nailing girls like that, they know they'll never be able to do the same, so no wonder they hate us, no wonder they want to take out our society. They're frustrated. A woman calms you down, calms all men down. Your aggression just leaks out of you between her legs. I remember reform school. Guys so mad they'd do anything, but they had us playing football and boxing, doing exercise twelve hours a day. That got rid of the anger. And anyway, we were so tired all the time we didn't have the energy to get mad. Then we were out in the big bad world and the first thing we do is get laid. Some of us hitch up with a broad, and it all calms down. The rage. Imagine if that deprivation went on into our twenties. We'd be the ones grabbing an AK47 and yelling for the blood of societies which got laid regularly. These guys, these Holy Warrior types, they're like bulls who can't get at the cows. Do you go in the field and try to pet the bull when he's got a hard on? No, of course not. You're nuts, I say.

But suddenly Johnny is starting to make sense here. I study his eyes for emotion but I see none. So what do you suggest? I ask. He grins, Let's try something, just for interest. I've thought about this for a while now. Don't tell the Colonel. Let's try some porn on our boy downstairs before he leaves us forever. Just for fun. We'll rest him and show him some tonight, whaddya say? A movie maybe. You crazy bastard, I say. But I'm thinking maybe Johnny's onto something here, and we never tried it before. We'll just call it R and R. Can't lose. Anyway, I wouldn't mind watching some porn. Then we'll kill the Pathan and incinerate him in the morning. Johnny m'boy, I say patting him on the shoulder, You're a fucking genius.

Back in The Room we see that our boy is in no state to watch a porn movie because he's dead. He died ten minutes ago, says Aktar the guy who tends the jail. Get rid of him and bring us another, I say. Aktar yells for a lackey down the corridor and a few minutes later they wheel the dead man away. They clean the floor and bring a new man. As is our custom he is chained naked to a wheelchair. Welcome to The Room I say, and the translator translates. The man says nothing. He looks exactly like the last, huge, muscular, bearded. His eyes are slits behind bruised puffy cheeks. Welcome to America, I say as we position him in front of the 80 inch VCR screen we use for psychological interrogation. The man stares at the blank screen. Welcome to Hollywood, says Johnny, tweaking the prisoner's cheek, slipping a video into the machine. He switches it on and we sit back to watch. We're drinking whiskey, John Jameson and Son. A young girl, blonde, sixteen, seventeen maybe, is standing in a room. She is watching herself in the mirror. She runs her hands over her white blouse, undoing the buttons, her hands slipping under her bra. She moans and lies down pulling her shirt open while her other hand slides down her leg, then up under her short red tartan skirt. She pulls the pin away from the kilt so that her legs are free. Her fingers press over the soft material of her panties, then over the elastic rim, underneath, slipping inside. She cries out, pushing the panties down. Johnny and I are so absorbed that we forget our boy in the wheelchair for a while until we hear a roar of rage. He's struggling, yelling, foam spraying over his vast beard. Will you look at that, say's Johnny, sipping his whiskey. I start to laugh hysterically. The prisoner's dick is standing upright like a guardsman, from out of a jungle of curly black hair, every blood vessel straining. I can see the tendons in his neck like ropes under the skin. His arms and legs are lined with sinews about to pop. He's grinding his teeth, struggling so hard that he's cutting himself on the chains. He tries to shut his eyes but the girl's moans make him look. Her fingers are dipping in and out of her pink hole, a hint of moisture glistening. She starts to come, her cries more urgent, like the sounds of torture. I hear the prisoner grunting. Johnny and I are staring in disbelief. We've both got woods but nothing like this guy. Gripped by spasms the prisoner ejaculates, big gobs of spunk leaking like ectoplasm over his legs and thighs. Enough to fill up four and twenty virgins. The spasms gradually cease, his dick begins to wilt, and he slumps against the metal sides of the wheelchair. He's given up. We've broken him. The girl is lying on her front now, two fingers in her vage, while another eases into her butt. I drain my whiskey. We switch the machine off and turn on the lights. The prisoner is weeping. I look at Johnny and he looks at me. I think we're onto something here, I say. Yeah, says Johnny, Yeah. He stands in front of the prisoner and starts to laugh. Hey Aktar, I yell, Clean this mother up and put him to bed.

We try the same routine on six or seven Holy Warriors and the results are outstanding. Each time we break them, reducing them to sticky sniveling wrecks. Project XXX is born. This is the heart of counter espionage. Johnny and I clean up. We put on our best uniforms after requesting an audience with His Highness the Colonel. We type a report. The Colonel is naturally skeptical, that's his job, but after witnessing our work in progress he becomes one of the converts. War's a dirty business, he says sipping the JJS, It's amazing what it reduces you to. This is why true warriors never discuss their work. Yes, Colonel, I say saluting. Johnny is standing rigidly to attention as only a long serving enlisted man can. The Colonel clears his throat, I'm very proud of you boys. You both realize that this could win us the war? We hope so, sir, I reply. He salutes us, I'll be recommending you both for medals. That is all gentlemen. We salute, turn, and march out of the office.

Events move fast, just in time. The rebels are massing for an attack. Intelligence reports come back of thousands of troops supported by tanks and artillery. Our bombers sally forth to engage the enemy, but this time they're not dropping bombs. Bombs have never done any good. No better than pissing on a wasps nest. Instead, the loaders stuff packages of hardcore porn into the bomb bays, Hustler,

Penthouse, Knave, heavy duty unmarked Danish, Dutch, and Swedish magazines. Even a little child porn slipped in without the General's knowledge. He's got a political career to look forward to, and we don't want to get him into trouble. The planes take off saluted by the Senior Staff. The Air Force's finest mission since Hiroshima, every crew member a hero for the cause. We hear them receding into the distance. They unload their cargoes in front of the rebel lines and return after an hour with the loss of only one aircraft. The top brass watch the results through huge night glasses as the rebels emerge after dark to see what the white barbarians have dropped. Johnny and I are honored guests. The General offers us a flask of JJS. With bated breath we observe, hoping for the best. It's our last chance.

Within minutes, fighting breaks out. A mullah is trying to stop robed troops from looking at the material but the soldiers push him over and start to fight amongst themselves even though they stand amidst thousands of porn mags. Hundreds of mujahadeen pour out of the trenches wondering what is going on. Could it be biological warfare? Have the white barbarians sent some drug that has made the Holy Ones go mad? Through the night glasses I see heaps of robes fighting for magazines. Shooting starts. From behind us I hear the moans and cries of a young girl. Phase Two of Project XXX. I turn round, pleasantly drunk from the whiskey. An enormous screen set up out of the rebels' artillery range. A young blonde lying on a bed, hips moving slightly, her manicured fingers slipping between her legs. Her breathing and the music of her ecstasy echo across the vast bleak plain. A halfhearted burst of rocket fire approaches the city, falling short of our lines. Then silence. For the first time in many years there is no shooting. No artillery duels, no sniper fire, no rockets. Nothing. Thousands of men on both sides are watching a young girl fingering herself. Peace has come.

In the following days, our onslaught continued. The war petered out. Night time became a vast blue movie show and the day was spent recovering. The mujahadeen began to drift away from the lines in their thousands. They camped around the city in the hope of porn. Copies of Hustler became a new currency. The mullahs were all put to death. Within a couple of years, Afghanistan was fast becoming the sex capital of Central Asia. A vast dusty Amsterdam visited by British tourists and Germans, run by ex-mujahadeen dressed in expensive suits, providing the best pot on earth, beautiful women, and a meritocratic hardworking society based on the dollar.

Johnny and I were decorated for our services to freedom and democracy. But the war was over, there was no-one left to torture. Life became increasingly dull. We began to drink too much. Then one day, sitting outside a cafe in Kabul, downtown ritzy Kabul, Johnny says, Hey, listen up. How about getting into the movies? Whaddya mean ya crazy fuck? I reply. No seriously, says Johnny, Seriously, S and M, snuff movies, you know. It's the next big thing here, they haven't got there yet but soon they will. We can corner the market if we're quick. I think about this for a while and then I say, Johnny m'boy you're a fucking genius, you know that? A fucking genius, Johnny Scotland.

Snuff

The years go by, and Johnny Scotland and I settle in Kabul. We see the city grow. Gone is the pile of rubble we moved into after the war. Now there's a financial district, the stock exchange is power housing Central Asia, and former Talibs in Ralph Lauren T shirts and pleated pants are mowing their lawns, cleaning their SUVs on Sunday. Tourists come, for the climbing, the pot, the archaeological ruins, the porn. That's how Johnny and I made our money, we got in there early. Johnny was Mayor for two terms, he helped renovate the streetcars. We meet for a game of golf, we're members of the Armed Forces Club, and sometimes we sit with our Highballs talking about old times.

We both married local women, several of them actually. Our wives still wear burkas, for their own safety and ours, because they are so incredibly gorgeous underneath all that cloth that, if they didn't wear these garments, society would go mad. Like looking at the Shield of Athena. First time we ever saw them Johnny and I looked at each other and whistled. At that moment, we knew why the Taliban fought so hard. They didn't want outsiders shooting their muck into these broads.

And another thing, no-one could ever understand why the women didn't struggle to be liberated. We had gender experts, lesbian theorists, female cops, people from San Francisco working day and night to liberate these women to no avail. They simply did not want to be liberated. We began to understand when we started hanging out with the Talibs, the guys we were fighting, these guys told us everything. Finally, when we're hooked up with some of these gals, we understand even more. The women never go out because they like to stay at home. And when you marry a whole bunch of them, you suddenly find you are not the head of the household, the broads are. They run everything. They shop, cook, control the money, they argue you to a standstill because they never let up. You try arguing with seven or eight broads in burkas.

So the wealthier you are the less powerful you are because you have more wives than any man. It's a trap you're in before you know it. The average Joe thinks, Hey, I can have lots of women, therefore I'm a real man, so he goes out and gets himself a harem. But lo and behold, he has to satisfy them too, and that ain't easy, and if he doesn't, well, they never leave him alone, or they'll find other men and destroy his life. Then there are feuds, duels, it's happened between harem endowed Americans here, but isn't Texas like that, or Utah? Hasn't it always been like that pretty much anywhere? But there's a sweet side too. The more powerful you become the more women you have, the more you can be a little boy in shorts again.

Hey, welcome to the history of Afghanistan. We've been absorbed, we're living it, the history of the country in a nutshell. Who's conquered who? It might explain why Afghan men have always been happier in the mountains killing each other. And these broads, they hang out together smoking hashish in the cool of the house, lounging about listening to the peacocks and the mina birds, watching the fountain. They don't have to go through all the shit of having to go the mosque. And who's out there doing all the work in the cauldron of midday? Who has to go to the mosque all the time? The guys of course, the losers in this whole damn thing. Maybe we should have been liberating them. Tell that to the Army boys in Alabama, Georgia, Mississippi. When I realized this, I shed tears. We'd been fighting people for nothing. And why were the Taliban so tough? Well, they had nowhere to go, nothing to do, except loose off their guns and get rid of all the anger either because they didn't have any women, or else they had too many. Johnny and I woke up to this way late, when we both had harems. Now we seldom go home except to fuck, eat, and sleep. And we've got so many kids I only know the names of a dozen. And yeah, Johnny and I like to roam around with machine guns shooting at stuff now and then.

The movies are what made us rich. We cornered the market, got into niches at the right time, porn, all types, fetish, regular, teen. We did other stuff too, ads for soap, cars, shaving cream, you name it.

But the snuff movies made us the big bucks. With our background in torture, we were poised to dive into the perfect market. Here's how it goes. Real snuff movies are, for obvious reasons, hard to come by. The true connoisseur knows the genuine article, they horde them like gems. And when you encounter a really good one, a work of art, as opposed to the crap the Russians produce, it will cost you a hell of a lot. Making them's easy enough. Especially with a war. People are free, you just go out in a limo, find someone you like, feed them, coax them with dollars and a story about Hollywood, take them back to the studio, get the camera ready, do the biz. Now it's a tad harder, with all the peace. You have to look around, and we only do beautiful people.

Johnny and I work for some high rollers who want their snuff movies tailor made. We get an order from one of our regulars. He stipulates, I want you to make me a snuff movie with a 1920s setting, nice young French girl, then he specifies the statistics he wants, blonde, nice titties, bobbed hair. And the background, It has to be in a hotel, he continues, Plush, she has to be dressed as a maid, she has to be murdered with a cutthroat razor, a slick of arterial blood has to be in her hair etc. Or whatever the punter wants. Johnny and I get on our merry way to seek out the fair maid and put the whole shebang together. Down the line we get it right, no second chances, you only get one chance at killing, and the experts can spot a duff snuff movie like jewelers can tell a fugazi diamond. There are duffs out there who fluff it, they try to kill a corpse twice, then it's just comedy. No escaping the punters, they get wind of this and the duffs get snuffed. When it's all set up, the customer gets the movie with rights of copy, we keep another for the archives. Johnny and me, we're the top of the Pyramid, but there's one eye.

One of our best customers is the General. He's the guy who won the war here. He got his five stars, he went into politics, now he is a big shot in the National Security Council. Forget the President, he's the patsy, if he doesn't behave he'll get snuffed. It's the NSC boys who run the show. The General never forgot us. We get Christmas cards from him, occasionally he'll visit for a little R and

R, play a game of golf, indulge himself in some live stuff. He loves to kill little girls, after having his way with them. Nothing under the age of eleven, mind, he abides by his codes. Everyone respects his restraint. Boys, he drawls, If it weren't for you, I'd still be living in a barracks in some far place, Guantanamo Bay maybe, yearning for the big time, longing for home. I'll never forget you, any time you need something, just give me a call. Johnny always jumps straight to attention when the General says this. Stiff as a ramrod, Johnny's kept himself in shape, it's a wonder to see. Yes sir, General, sir, he snaps, saluting. At ease, soldier, says the General.

Oh, the time goes by, easy street, and Central Asia's ours, we're the first people to control the region since Alexander the Great. The money rolls in, everything as good as it could ever be, the years pass. Investments grow, the USA is the biggest empire the world has ever known, the people are happy. Too damn happy, complains the General, If anything ever goes wrong they'll be too damn soft to defend themselves. This country's starting to remind me of a pond in summer. We need violence godammit, some evolution. Not like the old days. I remember when . . . and he goes into a monologue that can last for hours, seems like the General lived the entirety of US history. People drop off to sleep, or fetch themselves another whiskey, JJS of course, like medieval England where all day Sunday church attendance was obligatory, but you could slip out for a pint now and then, why so many pubs are within walking distance of a church. I found this out when Johnny and I were based in East Anglia during the Cold War. We were working on East Germans using tricks their fathers taught us … And that's how this country became the greatest country on earth, the General concludes, having compared the Greeks, the Romans, the Arabs, lambasting the British, lampooning the Turks, diminishing the French and the Germans, ridiculing the Spanish and the Italians, let alone the Russians, the Portuguese, and the Chinese. How the Red Indians were a bunch of primitives who needed to be wiped from the face of the earth, My great great Granddaddy was a sergeant under George Armstrong Custer at the Little Big Horn, he drones, Tragedy we didn't finish them off, godammit, the sons of bitches, I could use for hunting some of that prime reservation land those alcoholic savages own. The General pauses for a sip of JJS. Yes sir, General, sir, everyone shouts, Absolutely sir.

Then one day on the edges of the empire, in a distant land named Balustan, the natives topple the king. We see shaky footage of the mob invading the palace, the king seized along with his family. We see the mob setting fire to the palace, lynching the royal family, dancing in the streets. Naturally, some of the natives do not agree with these procedures, very soon a civil war erupts. Johnny and I watch events with mild interest, more for entertainment than anything else. The royalists are put to death, the revolution is complete. The revolutionary government builds a new palace, enforces new codes of behavior, new dress codes, everyone has to wear pajamas, not Maoist pajamas, rather striped pajamas from British styles of the 1920s, the trousers with drawstrings. They start to rebuild. These people are hostile to us, but they pose no immediate threat. However, I'm starting to think, and I feel Johnny's on the same radio channel, we start to look at each other in strange ways. He looks away and simpers, I wonder what's up. I blush. We get confused, down the line both of us admit that we suspected we were going gay. Then the General calls, and puts us straight.

Boys, he says, I've got a job for you. We sit in the VIP room of the Kabul Hilton sipping our whiskey, and the General starts to explain. We need this country, boys, Balustan I believe it's called, a fine god fearing country and we're gonna get it. Hell, we could go in right now, take it in a few weeks. We need it because if we don't get it, the Russians will, or the Chinese, who knows even the British. We're going to do these monkeys a favor, invade them before they get invaded by someone else. I heard they have to wear 1920s striped British pajamas, with the drawstring. Isn't that reason enough, fer chrissake? Donate them everything American, all the trimmings, all our values, everything free of charge. Problem is, how do we get the great American people to support the project? I don't know what the hell's wrong with everybody. He stares, one eye twitching.

The General is right. This has got to be the laziest goddamn empire in history. But why should the American people want to participate in such a project? The problems are thousands of miles away. Things are going fine, everyone's rich, who wants fine young sons going off to fight in some lousy swamp, when they could be going to college to study business, maybe even get an MBA? But if we don't get this country, someone else will, and that's how empires start to collapse. General, sir, says Johnny Scotland, Excuse me for interrupting sir, I'm thinking Czechoslovakia, 1938.

Shaking, the General ejaculates, Exactly, exactly, you took the words right out of my mouth, son. And that's where you boys come in. You're going to make a movie. A movie, sir? asks Johnny. A movie, the General repeats grinning, What you boys do best, a snuff movie. With a star cast of select US military personnel. Special Forces dressed as Balustanis. They attack our borders, you film the action, we show it to the American people, they get mad enough to support our project, we invade. As simple as that. Just like the Germans with Czechoslovakia. You hit the nail, Johnny Scotland. Get working boys, we need results fast before those goldarned liberals get the upper hand in Congress.

The mechanism starts rolling, the cameras in the exact same spots we'd place machine guns, we know our terrain Johnny and I, we capture events. It's always odd to see our own people getting blown to smithereens, machine gunned, bombed, but it's all on film, it's a movie after all. Hey, it's not the first time we did this, it sure won't be the last. One of the oldest tricks in the book, and it works, part of the game. The Great Game, the Brits called it. And these martyrs will be heroes, they'll be immortalized, like the boys at Pearl Harbor, the folks in the Twin Towers. Every year their names will be honored, we'll have shaped another keystone of the great American myth.

Headlines around the world explode. The liberals fade into the background, they go into exile in Holland, or they jump onto the roller coaster of war. The American people are motivated all right. Furious grandpas try to enlist, flexing biceps, dying their hair, thousands of young men rally to the flag, girls only date a fellow if he's wearing a uniform. Sports stars motivate the masses. Oh there are pockets of protest, the usual places, San Francisco, New York, the peaceniks forgetting, as usual, that they are just as invested in this as we are. It's in our interests to leave them alone. They have the joy of their illusions because we're so fucking strong the barbarians are very far from the gates. I mean, how many people in history had the luxury of voting, and protesting, and planning their retirement?

"Evolution Not Revolution," is the General's motto, and he's content. The USA is strong in its resolve, we're worth many millions more. It's going to be a long war. We've got stakes in companies linked to military supply, we'll make a killing. And we're directing The Movie. Along with the General, Johnny and I are among the most powerful people on the planet, the Eye in the Triangle. E Pluribus Unum. Reform school boys made good, Johnny and I are living the dream. We meet the General in his New England retreat. The butler takes us down the long polished corridors of the labyrinthine manor to the parlor where, as he is accustomed in his leisure time, the General is dressed as a 17th Century English Civil War cavalier. He offers us JJS, on the rocks of course. With boys like you, the General enunciates, This country will always be great. We salute, shouting, Yes sir, General, sir. At ease, soldiers, he growls. He takes a little silver box from his pocket, opens it and, placing white powder between his thumb and his forefinger, he sniffs it up one nostril then the other. Johnny and I look at each other amazed. We haven't seen the General doing coke for more than twenty years, not since the Central America business. He observes us then, in Queen's English, with a touch of Old Etonian, he says, Snuff, old chap, snuff. Fancy a pinch?

The Monkey House

Mensforth smiled, sweeping back his white hair, So as you are well aware gentlemen, we are under siege, our position is precarious. Thought policing is in a relative infancy, but what we know will ensure our immediate survival. I congratulate you upon your selection, you will carry the torch. The technology is implanted in your brains, and you will begin training. I wish you a very good afternoon, and again I welcome you. Some call this place the SPAR, the School of Psycho-Anatomical Research. Others have termed it the Monkey House. Interpretations are subjective. In essence, it is a university within the university.

He paused, scanning our faces, I'm sure I don't need to reiterate to you, after your experience in the field, there is no such thing as right or wrong. Completion of the goal is the sole factor, finish the job by any means at your disposal. And lastly, as you may already know, there's a documentary. You may find it useful, you're not obliged to attend, of course, but it's highly recommended you do. Those interested please proceed to the Queen's Theater. He bowed slightly, turned his back on us, and left the room. I glanced at Baxter, Ready? Yes, he replied, jamming papers into his briefcase, Let's go. The others left while I waited. Baxter, I'd known him for years. We were at Corpus, then we served in the Guards. After special ops we were assigned to Whitehall.

We descended the stone stairs. I have a feeling about this, he ventured. Oh, we'll muddle through, old chap, I interrupted, Just an extension of what we've been doing, albeit in a new realm. He smiled, I rather liked what Mensforth said about Machiavelli. Our glorious liberal empire, I laughed, shrugging my shoulders, Well it's true, Old Nick's always there in some form or another, but this time it's different. I mean no marks on the body, the public don't know, we can do what we want, absolutely anything. I heard rumors but I thought it was gossip, Baxter muttered, The potential is staggering, warfare of the mind, we're on the frontier. Exactly, I replied, Like

Romans looking north into Caledonia, remember the Ninth Legion. Nothing guaranteed.

We strolled across the quadrangle, the fountain splashing in the weak autumn light. The lawn where Marlowe walked. It really could make us invincible, he continued, For a while at least, I'm intrigued, and hitherto no ill effects from the procedure. How about you? Absolutely, I agreed, I'm tip top, never felt better. Have faith, old chap, we'll be invading dreams. And we'll have the luxury of dictating the battlefield. Look, we'd better hurry if we're going to catch that film. Then we can relax, maybe have a beer later. We probably won't have much time after today, I've a feeling this might get rather tough. Baxter smiled, Good idea, strange to be here again, Stanforth, isn't it? Yes, I said, Very odd.

We hurried through the medieval passages. A hint of frost, the first breath of winter. We were just in time. We entered, pushing into cavernous musty darkness past a red velvet curtain. Aside from a man in a trilby wearing an overcoat, seated in a distant balcony, the only people in the auditorium were two of the students. One of them waved. Where is everyone? I muttered. Baxter nodded. The light flickered and we settled in our chairs. Grainy black and white film. The opening scene a cinema, a man in a hat and an overcoat, two others, two young men seated together. Astonished, I raised my hands, as did one of the characters in the film. The man rose on screen. Bowing elaborately, leaning over, he removed the trilby, casting away the overcoat. Mensforth. What on earth is going on? Baxter yelled, his voice echoing through the auditorium. Mensforth laughed, his teeth huge, his face spreading across the horizon, Not of the earth, old fellow, rather the mind. Hasten not away because there is no exit. The show has commenced, you are the movie, your training has begun. In order to break people you have to be broken, you have to know from within, intimately, the process of breakdown, from misery cometh mastery. Do I really have to explain? We will focus on trauma, like our dental colleagues with an exposed nerve. We are within, we will show you. Through the implants we know everything from the day you were born, we own you. Stately, he waved shouting, Maestro. The film changed to color. The students walked out of the cinema. Colleagues to entice you, Mensforth chuckled, We'd have got you sooner or later, if you'd decided to slack tonight. To catch a duck, you lie for hours in a boat, 12-bore loaded, dummy ducks floating about the water. Eventually, the ducks come.

Images of our past sped across the screen, childhood, first days at boarding school, beatings, a bully's smile, nightmares, the implants seeking experiences from which we had not recovered. The pictures slowed, focusing. Willows, a Tudor cottage, summer idyll. A young boy in shorts, Baxter kneeling in the corner of a wine cellar. A hand sliding honey over an erect penis, Come on, come on sonny, suck the lollipop, you told me you like honey, suck it, suck it boy. Baxter leaning forward, rose bud lips parting. Next to me, Baxter was shaking, muttering, No, oh no, no. Keep your mind Baxter, it's all right, I whispered, For God's sake, it's training. God, you say, God, Mensforth chortled. He staggered, hiccupping, clutching his throat, Ggggod, gggggod. Burping, he cleared his throat, fanning himself, A word, an utterance, a sound produced by stimuli, recognized the same way, muscular contractions driven by electricity and chemicals, one could go on. He cackled, A voice crying alone in the wilderness, I am God, so are you, the figment of ourselves created in God's image, the comedy's divine, dissolve gentlemen, reform, for you are the stars.

My aunt was playing the harpsichord in the study. My mother slurring words, drinking scotch in the rancid afternoon light. I was on leave after months living in a badger hole watching IRA men. We were sitting in deckchairs in the garden. I took a deep drag of the cigarette. She smiled, You were an accident one could say, you ruined our lives, a night of lust in front of a fire, the beast with two backs, never ever have children, please, you never get over them they're with you forever, oh all the things I could do, could have done, I wanted to be a nun, I wish I'd been a man, I was going to dance, but no, you came along, and that was that, and you're so ungrateful. I heard myself shouting, A mother's love is unconditional. My mother cutting, Nothing is unconditional, love is a transaction like anything else, your father would agree if he were alive, I was the trophy he had the money. Squashing the cigarette, I stared at her, the sunglasses hiding my tears. Men in their thirties weren't supposed to cry, especially spies, the memory flooding through me like a polluted tide. You can't hide, she sniped, You really can't hide, you're unloved, unwanted, a zero, totally alone, you come into this world alone, you leave on your own. She drained her glass, As the odds go, you'll be another statistic, a suicide, just like your father.

I tried to stand, but I found myself paralyzed. Don't think you can flee, Mensforth boomed, It's all in the mind. And where do you think you'll go? You are the stars, the last of a long process, think of the taxpayers, they get their money's worth. Or I lose my job. And I was fingering Charlotte, one finger, two, then fucking her, Baxter's fiancée, the afternoon in my rooms, the camera closing on my buttocks moving between her legs. Late summer death in the air. Baxter never found out, he married Charlotte in September. Her cries echoed through the cinema. My bowels moved, a feeling of vertigo, I vomited over my knees. You'll have to kill me, you bastard, Baxter whispered, struggling in the seat unable to move, You thieving swine. Because if you don't you're going to die. Exactly, and I support you old chap, let battle commence, Mensforth encouraged, Like knights of old. No holds barred. Actually, he continued, Actually, very hush hush, obviously we didn't tell you this, the process is so secret it is permissible that only one of you survive. Natural selection good sirs, I'm sure you understand. You are the last, you have reached the top of the pyramid, and there is room for one. One eye in the Triangle, I'm sure you understand.

I opened my eyes. Flies. The hospital silent. Ward D1, we'd received the implants. The bed next to me labeled Baxter was empty. My hair matted with blood, left ankle broken, I crawled towards the corridor. The floor sticky with gore, the stench like a latrine in summer. I stared into the next ward, wondering why I was still alive. Medical personnel slumped, throats sliced, as though a mechanical scythe had butchered. Baxter's methods, I had to get out. I heard a repetitive thumping. A nurse jammed the automatic lift, her battered head striking the ceiling. Throat cut like a big red smile. Someone was singing, Here's to the road a whisky knock it down knock it down, here's to a whisky knock it down knock it down. Baxter loved single malt, he was coming up the stairs. I hid, squinting round the corner. Jauntily, he strode down the corridor whistling, soaked in blood, a huge amputation knife in his beefy fist.

Rain lashed the window panes, the wind howling through the trees. What happened, Charlotte whispered, switching on a light, What is it? Baxter, I hissed, waking drenched in sweat, Baxter, the hospital, he came up the stairs. But he's away, Charlotte soothed, It was only a dream. Go back to sleep, Darling, everything's fine, he'll never know. I watched myself curled in bed, Charlotte caressing my face. At the end of the aisle, Mensforth smiled, smoking a cigarette, The brain resembles Africa, it is shaped much the same. He tapped a diagram, If one includes the spinal cortex. Africa in the 1870s, we know the coast relatively well, but the interior remains unexplored, you are traveling to the heart of a continent gentlemen, remember Burton and Speke. Neither man ever the same again, what they encountered, they became deadly rivals. Speke committed suicide. Where lies the source of the river? The river of consciousness running from the great subconscious lake. We will fight them in realms we know through our dreams. The mind our colony, the sun never setting for it will never rise, the empire darkness, and it will be endless. He chuckled, The universe within the universe, we will will the Will. Baxter stared, his face ivory, beads of sweat dropping to his suit. The film flashing over his pupils. He was far away, searching for me.

When Baxter reached the end of the corridor, he turned and announced, I know you're there Stanforth, you bitch's bastard, I'm saving you till last, I will enjoy you at my leisure, I will gut you like a trout. Retching, I struggled in the slime, not knowing where I was going or how I had arrived. Mensforth's voice droned through the hospital, The game isn't over till the whistle, play up, play up, play the game, it's not the winning that matters, old chap, it's the taking part, British spirit, what, remember who you are, you're an Englishman, England's whitest, England's finest, an Englishman is the finest fellow in the world. Believe what you do, and you'll believe who you are. The far wall telescoped into a screen, a film showing grainy black and white. I saw myself sitting in the lecture room with Baxter and the other candidates. Mensforth was smiling, finishing the welcoming lecture.

Apes

We were in the highlands, surveying for uranium, my first time in the region. We had a few days off for Christmas, and Caruthers wanted to show me some good trout streams. He turned the spit, fat sizzling into the fire. How is it? he asked. Much better than one might expect, I replied. He tore meat from the leg, Unlikely to be a market for it back home, but it is usually quite good.

We shot the chimp just before sunset. We'd been watching them through the trees. They were agitated, screaming, shaking branches. Incredible, Caruthers muttered, I've only seen it a couple of times before, they're trapping Colobus monkeys. He passed me the binoculars, See for yourself. I scanned the foliage, focusing on a large male high in the canopy. He cornered a monkey. The monkey bared its teeth snarling, but it was no use. The chimp seized it by the neck, killing it instantly. Then it ravaged the nest throwing babies to the ground. Younger chimps grabbed the corpses. The big male descended the tree, dropping onto the leaves. He tore the Colobus to pieces.

We'll have to mention it when we get back, said Caruthers, You know, I don't think anyone's officially recorded such behavior, they're supposed to be vegetarian. Yes, I agreed, Everyone thinks they're friendly. Caruthers let out a shout of laughter, I remember in the Congo, they used to put prisoners in a cage with a male chimp, a few minutes later there wasn't much left of the poor fellow, first thing they do is rip off the testicles. Come on, let's catch supper, he whispered, Make them wonder who's in charge, develop their brains. He aimed, shooting the head off a young male. Nice shot, I said. The troop ran away screaming. He patted the .303, I've sometimes thought, that's the way it is. I mean, here we are wandering about in tune with our lives, or so we think, but we're in the crosshairs, just a matter of time. He pointed to the sky. I've never really thought about it quite like that, I replied.

After gutting the chimp, Caruthers prepared the fire, while I set up the tent. The darkness came quickly, it was never really light in the jungle. Soon the flames were high enough to cook, the intestines crackling across the wood. We didn't bother skinning the creature, there was very little fat. The fire burned away the hair, the smell of roasting meat making my mouth water. We sat gnawing the flesh, with yam and onions in a soup. We could hear the civil war across the border, the pop of mortars. There they go again, said Caruthers, Right on time.

The Governor

I lit a cigarette, inhaling deeply. Reminds me, Caruthers continued, Do you remember Mike Carter, he was at Imphal? He motioned, By the way, do have a drop. I poured from the flask, sipping Glenlivet. I recalled a lean undergraduate with white hair, he'd been studying for the Church until he lost his faith. He suffered a nervous breakdown. Then along came the war. You mean Mad Mike Carter? He was a Trinity scholar. Caruthers nodded, The same fellow, I met him in Burma, he was one of the few people Wingate listened to. What of him? I asked, I've often wondered.

Caruthers chuckled, stoking the embers, He always loathed monkeys, said they reminded him too much of himself. After the war, he couldn't handle peacetime at all. His drinking became a problem, and he was thrown out of the army for fighting. I laughed, Fighting? Caruthers smiled, He punched a general. The Colonial Office rescued him. They sent him to the south east during the civil war because he knew the territory after his activities with the resistance. Actually they were jolly glad to be rid of him, and no-one else would go. He was always rather odd, I interrupted, An eccentric one could say. Caruthers nodded, Well Carter thrived, he became increasingly popular. He spoke the languages, settled all sorts of disputes. Carter had returned, the word spreading like a mantra. He traveled in a Silver Cloud. The natives had never seen anything like it. Soon, it seems, they were murmuring Khurt Ah. Khurt Ah? I asked. Caruthers frowned, Oh, Khurt Ah's a deity, a monkey god, he appears in troubled times, in the temples he's always carved from the finest ivory, the whiter the better. He's the moon, dancing with the sun, rolling the earth to the new dawn. So Carter became a primate of sorts, I observed. Caruthers grinned, spitting out gristle, Precisely, some say he knew all along what he was doing, others disagree. All the tribes revere Khurt Ah, the shamans predicted he would reappear because of the chaos. And to cap it all they found out Mike was born in the Year of the Monkey. The war fizzled out. He was the obvious choice for Governor, the

Crown lets him get on with it. The region's completely settled down, indeed it's prospering.

I gazed at the flames, the remains of the chimp smoldering, Almost enough to make one believe, peculiar how these things happen. Caruthers gestured, More? No, no thank you, I replied, I think this part was a little underdone. He leaned over, Here, let me turn it again for you. I handed him the meat. In the distance, bombing thumped through the valley, then I realized it was thunder. Storm, said Caruthers. Yes, I agreed, We'd better take cover.

Cross Words

One of the nastier Consulate duties. Yesterday I arrived in Fackalik, a remote island in the archipelago, to collect the body of a British citizen recently killed by a mob. Attacked for no apparent reason. One minute he was walking through the square, perhaps looking for a hotel, then he was crushed under a rain of sticks and stones. Most odd. Although strictly Muslim, the region had been quiet, relations with the foreign community were very good.

The corpse was unrecognizable, the only human reminders being the empty rucksack, torn Levis, a shredded bloodstained shirt. The logo still visible PRESIDENT BUSH IS A PRICK. Then I understood. Most unfortunate, I whispered to Ali Pornfateer, the chief of police, an old friend, A strange death. He nodded, Terrible, terrible. How could the young man have known, I added, Unless he knew the dialect? Indeed, agreed Ali, passing me a glass of mint tea, The will of God. I lit a clove cigarette, inhaling deeply, contemplating the parents. The address in Surrey. A quiet couple, believe in God no doubt, the father near retirement. I'm sorry to inform you.

In the sauna heat, I wait as they load the body into the jeep. Smoking a cigarette, I stare at the Grand Mosque, the beautiful calligraphy giving praise to God Almighty. The porters wave farewell with the ritual chant, Prick yet mung. God is everywhere. Prick yet mung, I reply, Prick yet fazeer, God is Great.

The Purveyor of Fine Toys and Games

We'd been there a couple of months, when one day I noticed a tall man in his early thirties walking quickly through the town. A white man. After a while you get used to the locals, so the sight of a tall white man strolling through streets was a newsworthy event. That evening back at the room I said to Gaz, Hey, guess what. What? asked Gaz, lying on his bed smoking a cigarette. I watched him for a few moments. I waited. He opened his eyes and looked at me. Come on then, he insisted, What, what happened? I grinned. I saw a white man, walking through the town, today. Oh yeah, he said sounding bored, exhaling smoke, What did he look like? I stood as though giving a lecture, He had a beard, a short beard, he was tall. He looked pretty tough. I think he was in his thirties. I've already seen him, said Gaz. When? I asked, offended he hadn't told me. Gaz laughed, In the cafe, a couple of days ago. He seems to be well known. He speaks good Spanish. I think he works here. But I don't know what he does. Why didn't you mention it? I asked. Gaz stubbed the cigarette, I forgot. I was going to, but I forgot. He closed his eyes, rummaging for another cigarette. I was fascinated to know who it was. Maybe he was British.

For several days, I looked for the man but I didn't see him. I began to think he'd just been a tourist on his way through the area. Then one day, about a week later, we were having breakfast at the cafe. We'd eaten the eggs and tortillas, and we were finishing our coffee. There he is, said Gaz, Don't look now, but he's over there behind you. Who? I asked. Gaz smiled, The Great White Hunter, the white man. I stood up. I'm going to the john, I announced. I walked past the rows of tables, hearing the animated chatter. I looked across the room, through the smoke. Sure enough, over by the far wall beneath the huge ornate mirror, I saw the fellow. He was sitting with two Mexicans, one broad and strong hunched over the table, the other slight with freckles and long eyelashes. They were drinking coffee, smoking cigarettes, studying a map. I strolled by, hoping that there might be some kind of recognition, but he either ignored me or he didn't see me. Then I thought maybe I didn't look white any more. We'd been insulted when we first arrived, clean shaven in our Levis and T shirts, we looked like American tourists. Hey, gringo, they yelled, Puto gringo. Several times this happened, and I grew nervous. They don't mean anything by it, Gaz said, trying to make the best of the situation, but we stopped shaving. We tried to look as poor as possible. We stayed in the sun all day, so we were tanned dark. The insults ceased the poorer and darker we became. Now I was unrecognizable.

After I pissed the coffee, I walked back, passing the table where the Great White Hunter was still talking with the two Mexicans. As I went by I said, How's the weather in London? The conversation stopped. They looked up saying nothing. I arrived at the table and sat down. What did you say to him? asked Gaz, He looked like he was going to kill you. I smiled, I asked him how the weather was in London. Gaz stared, Are you crazy? How do you know he's British? I don't, I replied, I didn't know what to say, I don't know anything, so I said the first thing that came into my head. It's rather like a spy film, where there's a code word or some motif that sets off the whole plot. Like The Third Man. You've been smoking too much of that stuff, said Gaz disgusted, You're losing it. You should see yourself, I countered staring at him, his bloodshot eyes, the lank dirty black hair hanging over his face, the scrofulous beard, You look like a flunky. He flinched, What's a flunky? I leered, I don't know, what you look like I suppose, you look like a flunky, go look in the mirror. He threw a cigarette at me and we finished the rest of the coffee in silence. We were getting on each other's nerves.

Another week passed, and no sign of the Great White Hunter. We began to speculate as to who he was. The tourist argument began to gain strength once more. Then we were in the cafe again one evening, drinking beer before dinner. We were discussing a game of cricket. The beer had gone to our heads, we were beginning to shout. So you guys speak English? I looked up. It was the Great White Hunter. Yeah, we both said. He grinned, Mind if I sit down?

No, no, go ahead, I stammered. I pushed a chair. He sat down slowly, careful to avoid spilling our beer. He tilted back his ten gallon hat. British? Yes, I said. You're American? Yup, Texas. I offered him a cigarette and he took one, lighting it with a zippo he extracted from his denim jacket pocket. He inhaled, slowly exhaling before asking, So what're you guys doing here in this part of the country, if you don't mind me asking? Don't see too many white boys around these parts. We're students, said Gaz, From Liverpool, we're here for a year abroad. The American exhaled again, smoke flooding from his mouth, Why d'you come here? We were sent, I said. Strange part of the country to come, he grinned, Not much going on around here. You could say that, I agreed, Maybe we should've gone to the DF. Maybe, said the American. You work here? asked Gaz. The American pushed his hat, Yup, been here for years, get back to Texas now and then, but I live here now. Like it too, it ain't so bad. I've got a wife and kids in Veracruz, another back in Texas, but my work's here for the most part. What do you do? I asked. His eyes narrowed, I work for the Governor, and I've got a shop, over on the other side of the cathedral. You guys should come and take a look some time. I was in the army, then I got married down here and started a shop. It's pretty good. I like it.

He leaned back in the chair, frowning, looking around to order a beer. Pursing his lips, he blew loud kissing noises. One of the waiters responded. An old man with a long mustache. Grinning, he came over. Three beers, on the double you lazy bastard, said the American. Everyone was grinning, and there was no malice. Puto gringo, said the waiter, You're nothing other than a puto gringo. He walked away yelling, Three beers, on the double for these sons of bitches. They're a good bunch around here, said the American, No problems. Better than up north. What do you guys think of the country? Pretty good, I said. Yeah, OK, agreed Gaz. We didn't mention the problems at the border, the menaces, the man trying pick a fight with us in full view of the police, being held at gun point the night they blew up the oil wells, the problems getting the tiniest amounts of money out of the bank. We didn't mention any of that.

We'd been trying to forget. We'd been trying to take it day by day. Yeah pretty good, I repeated, Not bad. That's good to hear, said the American, You can get into some scrapes if you're not too careful. But you guys look like natives. You always looked like that? No, said Gaz, We wanted to blend in, when in Rome, less problems that way. A wry smile, So you've had a few problems? I shrugged my shoulders, Oh, little things, at the border, you know, the usual. I was trying to be tough, trying to make the best of it. But we weren't fooling him.

He laughed, his tanned face creasing around the eyes. He shook a callused fist at us. This is what counts here, he said, The big stick. Violence. He laughed again, Mucho palo. We figured that already, said Gaz. The beer arrived, and the American paid. He thanked the waiter, who patted him on the back before leaving with his big silver tray. The American became serious, You'd better be careful, is all. Things sometimes happen. You never know. You've just got to watch out. If you have any problems, come and see me. I mean this. I can help you out. Any problems at all come and see me. Connections are useful here. You might need them some time. Everything's connections here, knowing the right folks. There's no other rule. Here's my card. I read James R. McKechnie III Purveyor of Fine Toys and Games. There was an address, a telephone number. Thanks, I said, We'll bear that in mind, I'm sure nothing'll happen. The American grinned, his cheekbones rising like Lee Van Cleef's. Let's hope not, he said, At least you speak the language. We raised our glasses, toasting each others health.

The American drained his glass in one and looked at his watch. Well, I've got to be going. Got to meet a little lady I know. He winked. Nice meeting you guys. No doubt we'll meet again. I'm sure we will, said Gaz. He had become rather subdued at the mention of trouble. The country had been getting to him, it seemed. All the time he was trying to make light of any problems that occurred but, since the night we'd been held at gun point, he'd appeared rattled. He was starting to drink a bit, his hands shook, he'd developed a taste for mescal. Some days he never left the room.

The American stood up and stretched, I'll be out of town for a while, got to visit the wife and kids. Have a good time, I said, We'll be around when you get back. The American raised his hat, So long boys. Looking like a gunfighter, he strolled out of the cafe after waving goodbye to the waiters. They shouted back, Hasta luego puto gringo. It was all very light hearted. Seems like a good guy, I said. Yeah, murmured Gaz, his face twitching, Sound as a pound.

The Toy Shop

Hey, come on in. The American beckoned, his teeth very white against a deep tan. We found the shop after a search of alleys north of the cathedral. He told us to visit, a message passed on by Pestañas. I wondered about his sense, running a toy shop in such an obscure part of town. But he knew what he was doing. He'd lived there for a long time.

How are you guys doing? Fine, I said, Fine. How about yourself? asked Gaz. Good, said the American, Just back from Texas. I told you I was traveling, didn't I? Well it was damn good to get out of this place for a while, gets to you. Know what you mean, muttered Gaz. He doesn't like it much, I said. Really? said the American, Trouble? Gaz nodded, Oh it's all right, takes a bit of getting used to. The American laughed, You're not the only one, different reality, different time. Mexican time. Too many Mexicaners for starters. Wish I could stay in Texas, but this place has its advantages. Anyway, come on in. He stared down the street at two men leaning against a wall. They grinned, one yelling, Puto gringo. He waved, Friends of mine, a couple of guys who work for me now and then. We entered the shop.

Here it is, this is it. He pointed vaguely. Wait here, hey sit down. I'll be right back. He disappeared into the back of the store through a mesh curtain of colored beads. I looked at the garish walls. A chandelier hanging above us. Hundreds of toys lining the shelves, steel chess sets, designer clocks, bright contraptions, steel decorations. I wondered how he made any money. I looked at Gaz, and he raised his eyebrows. All right, like I said, here we go, yelled the American returning with a rolled newspaper. We were sitting at a glass table in the middle of the room. Some people tried the door, a couple shopping. We're closed, shouted the American, Go away. The couple ambled on.

The American unrolled the newspaper revealing clumps and fronds of fresh marijuana. An odor of fermenting mint and newly mown lawn. He began to roll a Havana. This stuff is all right, he whispered, Not bad, it'll do, but tomorrow if you guys are around I'm going to get some more from someone I know, much better. This here weed is average. Bought it last week, and it's reasonable. Nothing special though. He lit the joint, inhaling twice, his head disappearing in a cloud. He passed the smoldering cigar to Gaz. Gaz puffed, coughing, handing it to me. I sucked, the cigar crackling like a bonfire, one more time, gagging, giving it to the American. He motioned to Gaz. Gaz shook his head, grinning vacantly, his eyes already glazed red. If this is average, I dunno what good is, he droned, his nasal Liverpool accent making us laugh. I'm all right too, I agreed, chuckling, Bloody good stuff, very strong actually. The American deposited the cigar in a huge conch shell that served as an ashtray. The room buzzing. About half the joint remained, the paper stained black from the tar. Some music, he announced, rolling his chair backwards. He switched on a system by the wall. Yoko Ono.

So how've you guys been? Oh, not much happening, I replied, Not much to report. The American smiled, No news is good news, is what I say. I got this album in Japan, Plastic Ono. You were in Japan? I asked. The American smiled, Yeah, a while ago, when I was in the Army. When did you leave? Gaz mumbled. The Army? Oh, about five years ago. Before that I was in Germany, before that was Nam. Gaz leaned forward, You were in Vietnam? The American lit a Marlboro, Yeah. Two tours. Long time ago, he added, exhaling a stream of smoke, Long time. So now you run a shop, I said. The American began to laugh uncontrollably. Did he say something? asked Gaz grinning. For a moment, I thought the American was crying. The shop, he chuckled finally, his eyes red streaming tears, The shop, those two sad fucking tourists. Bet you boys think this shop is weird. A bit, I agreed. The American pointed at a yellow spaceship alarm clock, I mean, who buys that, who the fuck would ever buy a piece of crap like that? He began to laugh again, tears running down his face. Then suddenly he was serious, his face deadpan. He stubbed the cigarette, his eyes narrowing. He wiped his face, And who gives a shit? It doesn't matter.

No-one comes here, ever, and why the fuck should they? Those two idiots just now are the first people who wanted to come here in over a month, maybe two, I don't fucking know, I don't give a fucking damn either. They were probably from California, where the fuck else would they be from? This place is appearances, impressions, is all.

He lit another cigarette, I know you boys won't talk, and it doesn't matter if you do, I really don't give a shit. I mean who the fuck are you going to talk to? I work for the Governor. Train the body guard, teach them how to shoot, that kind of thing, get them fit for duty. I'm an advisor. Interesting, I said. Oh, you know, it's slack, continued the American, Real slack, just a bit of fun, a fucking holiday, and I get paid. Title's Special Advisor, a bunch of crap. Only thing special about it is they pay me dollars and I do fuck all. Easiest work I ever did. Fucking siesta. The whole thing's a fucking game. Ever thought about that? Nothing to do. Take my boys out now and then into the mountains, let them blaze away with their guns, teach them how to fight, that sort of thing. Make 'em happy. They love noise. Nothing to it. I get a lot of free time. They're good boys, but you need to push them. And they need us here, man, they'd fucking fall apart without us, whole country would go down the fucking tube, it's just a step away, fucking funny farm. What was it Porfirio Díaz said? Poor little Mexico, so far from God, so near to the USA. Well, you know what? God ain't there and the USA is. Dig that. God bless America. Here the fuck we are, and we ain't going anywhere. Know what I mean?

Someone was knocking on the glass door. I looked round. A tall cadaverous Mexican youth grinning, standing in the entrance. Ramón, said the American. He stood up, leaned towards the door, and let the fellow in. Ramón, some friends, the American announced in Spanish. This boy's as dumb as a bastard, he added in English, But he's a good old boy aren't you Ramón. The youth grinned vacantly, not understanding. We acknowledged him. The American began to talk in dialect, something about tomorrow, a rollo, midday. The youth nodded. They shook hands, the Mexican waving as he left. The American shut the door, Did you see the size of his hands? Yeah, replied Gaz laughing, His hands. I noticed the hands, but I thought it was the marijuana. The American chuckled, Biggest hands you'll ever see, he should learn the piano. He's going to bring me another one of these tomorrow. The American indicated the newspaper. Best fucking news I ever had. But better, he emphasized, whistling, Much better. One toke stuff, absolutely kickass. Give you guys some, if you show. He sat down.

Yup, I'm the most useful guy you're likely to know in this here town, the back of beyond, the real boonies down here, fucking nowhere, you know what I mean. Out in the fucking badlands. Don't know what I'm doing here sometimes. I mean have you ever thought, where the fuck are we? What the fuck are we doing here? Used to be much worse though, a few years back. Cleaned the place up. But seriously, one sign of trouble, from anyone, you boys come see me, is that clear? Ain't having nobody push around a couple of good boys like you, 'coz good boys is what you are, I can see that. Thanks, I said, Appreciate it, I hope it won't be necessary. Gaz nodded, Yeah, thanks a ton. You never know, said the American, Just in case. It's good to have, that's the way it works down here. I'll help you out. If you can't find me go see Manuel. You know Manuel? No, I replied. The American motioned, The big fellow at the cafe, always with me, he's Manuel. Strong bastard. Once saw him kick the shit out of five guys. Any problems, if I'm not around, go see him. He'll help you out too, just say you know me. He's useful. Thanks, I repeated. Yeah, thanks, said Gaz.

The American shook his fist, That's the way it works here, rules're simple. Like I told you once before. We work together. Big stick. Mucho palo. There's nothing else. That's why this country's so goddamn simple. I'm only telling you boys this 'coz you're white. Least you ain't fucking Mexicaners. Know what I mean? We're in this together. And just to let you know I'm serious, I mean business, I'm not fucking around, look here at this. The American reached into his jacket, pulling out a revolver, a .38 by the look of it. He smiled, The look on you boys faces, what do you expect? I'm from Texas. Texas godammit. I had a great granddaddy in the Texas Rangers for Chrissakes. Scares the shit out of them if you wave that.

He placed the gun on the table next to the newspaper. No-one's going to fuck with you, now you know James R. McKechnie III. That's me. He held the joint and lit it, inhaling, holding the smoke. He passed it to Gaz. I declined when Gaz was done, I'm really stoned, couldn't handle any more, it's like standing over a chimney. I got there a while back, mumbled Gaz, Too much. So we'll meet tomorrow? the American asked. Sure, I replied. Yeah, why not? agreed Gaz. Good, then that's settled. You guys ever eaten fresh duraznos straight from the tree? I looked at Gaz, Can't say we have, you ever eaten duraznos? Duraznos? said Gaz. The American pointed vaguely, Tomorrow we'll go to the jungle and find some. Nectar of the gods, fruit of the country, a reason to live, like eating a woman. Duraznos. I know where some is. I've got a couple of days off. There's an old deserted farm way out there with trees. We'll take some of this stuff and go. I'll show you around. Sounds good, I said, So here tomorrow about midday? The American nodded, Yeah, midday.

We stood up unsteadily and shook hands. Yoko Ono screaming. It was already dark. Well, hasta luego amigos, drawled the American, Good of you boys to come by. Good to see some white boys in town after so long. Kinda gets to you, know what I mean? Gotta stick together. Hey, thanks for everything, I said. Yeah, thanks repeated Gaz. We waved and the American shut the door. The town spread across the hillside in the distance, points of light in the dark, the vast darkness of the jungle beyond. The men we had seen earlier were still there. One of them yelled, Puto, puto gringo, gringo cabrón. Ignoring them, we walked away. Looks like a model, said Gaz, Like a model railway or something. Yeah, I agreed, A cartoon, not quite real, like those paintings done with dots.

The Big Man

I read the telegram. Marshall dead. Proceed Port Campbell immediately. So Marshall was dead. One of our best men. I lit a cigarette, wondering how he might have died. There had been an outbreak of cholera recently. I knew he hadn't been well. Poor old Marshall. I remembered a large fellow, clipped mustache, very English. My wife brought whisky. I have to go to Port Campbell, I said, Marshall's dead, I've got to close the negotiations. She paused for a few seconds, Oh dear, how awful. How long will it take? I don't know, I replied, A couple of days perhaps. I stared into the dark, the oil lamp flickering in the slight breeze.

Marshall had been very close to concluding the business. A matter of formalities. The consortium was about to control a quarter of the region's gold. We were going to mine an area bigger than London. Negotiations to resolve, apparently some of the natives' demands were still creating problems. I leaned towards the window. Below, jungle as far as I could see. The plane rocked and jolted, falling a few hundred feet. The pilot leaned round grinning, Sorry mate, storm ahead, we should make it, if not we'll put down in Zindawa. I nodded. Parts of the land were still unexplored, there was so much potential. In the distance, beyond the Jirian range, heavy black clouds seethed with the light of a vast storm. The plane banked and we flew in the opposite direction. The pilot shouted, Slight diversion mate, we don't want to be over there. I nodded again. Leaning back in the seat, I felt the sweat dripping down my face. I took two mouthfuls of whisky from the flask, followed by a long drink from the water bottle. Twilight came fast, the sky flaming red then dark blue. I dozed.

A shout interrupted a dream of fly fishing in Scotland, Nearly there. I rubbed my eyes. We were circling. Port Campbell below, capital of the northern region, just a few shacks and a hotel. Towns meant nothing here. Three dirt roads to nowhere, a vast blackness beyond, and the river, its source in the western highlands. Far to the south, the sky periodically lit up like a huge theater. We landed, bumping heavily a couple of times. I thanked the pilot and staggered out of the plane. A huge figure was walking towards me. Caruthers? Yes, I replied. Name's Brodrick, Moss Brodrick. We shook hands. You're lucky to be here. The storm, he added, Should arrive tonight. We climbed into the jeep.

We sat in my room, the fan creaking above us, outside a torrent of rain. Be like this for a few hours, said Brodrick, Nothing else to do but down more of these. He pointed at the beer. Well, I suppose we'll have to make the best of it, I said. We sat in silence, the heat rendering all movement absurd. So Marshall, how did he die? I asked. Brodrick exhaled smoke, handing me another bottle, It was a game. A game? Yes, he continued, Christmas Day, they were playing a game. Who? I interrupted. Oh, some planters and Harry Morgan, he's a local trader, well, he drinks a bit you know, and they like to rib him now and then. That night they were putting a dead snake on his car roof, and when old Harry left the bar to drive home of course he saw the snake. So he dashed back into the bar yelling about a snake on his car. Everyone laughed and said, You're drunk old man, seeing things again. Marshall nipped outside and removed the snake, so when everyone went to see what Harry was on about naturally there was no snake. Harry had one more for the road, Marshall put the snake back, and the same thing happened, Harry came running in again scared out of his wits. They repeated the joke several times until Harry was frantic. The last time Marshall went out to remove the dead snake to give Harry a rest, there was a real snake, it bit him. Northern Taipan, must've fallen from a tree. He was dead within minutes. They thought it was his heart till they saw the fang marks, unmistakable. Poor old Marshall. And it finished off Harry, he left for England. Good God, I said. Brodrick turned and stared through the window at the rain, Yes, most unfortunate. By the way, this might slow us down, but things should clear. I suggest we get some rest, you must be exhausted. Good idea, I agreed. Stay in the room, he added, Keep the door locked, and here, take this. He handed me a .45. Haven't seen one of these since the war, I said. Where were you? he asked. North Africa mainly, how about you? Sweat dripping down his face, he stared, Burma, then here. He waved and closed the door. I washed, climbed onto the rickety bed, and fell asleep lulled by the crashing of the rain, the .45 on the floor.

A knock on the door. I touched the gun, Who's there? A deep voice, Big Man him wanna you eat breakfast. Footsteps down the corridor. The rain had stopped. I opened the blinds. Dawn, the end of the storm, retreating clouds penetrated by daggers of light. The air reeking of hot soggy vegetation. I could see the blue lines of the highlands a hundred miles to the north. A rooster pecked at the mud.

Brodrick was seated in the dining room, drinking tea. I hope you'll forgive me, I already ate, hope you slept well. Thank you, I said, Like a log. Master Number One ready now, Brodrick shouted suddenly. A hulking native emerged from the kitchen. He placed a plate on the table and served a four inch Witches Grub, fried to perfection. Looks good, I said. This wallah fine man, said Brodrick. The native grinned and bowed. Well, dig in old chap, then I'll fill you in on what's happening. Good idea, I mumbled. I chewed the soft meat, relishing the smoky aftertaste. Brodrick lit a cigarette, inhaling deeply. It's very simple. Every member of the tribe wants a bungalow, a lawn, some gardening equipment, especially lawn-mowers, and money to invest. I want the best for them, I hate to see them lose out, they helped us in the war you know. I recommended five hundred pounds each. Should see them through, they're all dead by forty anyway. Marshall was very against it for some reason. Is that all? I asked. Yes, Brodrick replied, You need to drive up country with me and sign with the chief. I'll be there, of course, you wouldn't make it alone. The missionaries send volunteers but they eat them. Nice fat missionary roasting on a fire. Have you ever seen that? No, I replied, Never. You get used to it, said Brodrick, First ate human in the war, thought it was monkey till they told me it was Jap, liver's the best part. Why do they leave you alone? I asked. Brodrick laughed softly, I'm the beer man, Imperial Breweries. I bring their beer, manna from heaven. We brew extra strong lager especially for them, sold nowhere else. Keeps them happy. It's currency, they treat it like gold. You know what they say? No, I said. He watched me, searching for signs of unease, Strong man strong beer. Come on let's get going, we must be back before night.

The village was a three hour drive through an emerald landscape, the grass lush with the recent rains. Trees laden with fruit, insects, brightly colored butterflies the size of dinner plates. Birds of Paradise. Brodrick was right, I could not have done the journey alone. We passed tribesmen carrying spears, naked except for penis horns, bones through their noses, their bodies muscled like Greek statues. Very few whites had ever been this far. They watched suspiciously until they saw Brodrick, then they cheered, running alongside the jeep mile after mile. We were towing a trailer crammed with beer. By the time we reached the village, sixty or seventy warriors surrounded us. Brodrick stopped the jeep and yelled, Where is Big Man One Talk? Take me to One Talk Big Man. The tribe sighed as one, a vast exhalation, as a very old man was lifted towards us on a chair, carried by six men their hard bodies caked in gray ash. One Talk Big Man me lug beer, Brodrick ranted, Strong man beer for big men. The old man gestured towards me, What name belong him? This man Master Number One, him Big Man too, friend of King. Pressed by the tribe, we followed the old chief to the long house, the interior lit by a single animal fat candle that sputtered in the breeze, the yellow light flickering over hundreds of skulls lining the walls. For a long time Brodrick lapsed into pidgin, the old man nodding occasionally, then he produced a document with the King's seal. All in order, he whispered, You just sign. I duly scrawled the quill over the parchment. Now we give them the beer and we leave. We want to be well away before nightfall.

I smoked a cigarette while warriors unloaded the beer. Brodrick stood while other warriors presented him with gifts, a twelve foot dead cobra, piglets, young girls, mirrors, a pack of cards. I stared across the countryside imagining the mine in a few years, the biggest in the world, and it would be ours. Poor old Marshall would be have been pleased. Pity about the view, but there was plenty more land, heavens, we'd only just started exploring the place. The

Japs had tried to take it and now it was ours, we'd got there before the Americans. Who knows what lay beyond? If they wanted bungalows, lawns, lawnmowers, a few hundred pounds, they'd bloody well have them. I watched a group of monkeys in some nearby trees. A dominant male was pursuing younger members of the troop. Fitzroy's Macaques, said Brodrick, following my gaze, That one's the Big Man. Sometimes, I wonder what the hell we're doing, he continued, Damn pity how it's all going to change, with the mine, I was really quite attached. There's bags more land, I replied, You can always move up country if you want. But the monkeys aren't giving up their trees for bungalows and lawnmowers, are they? he interrupted, And they couldn't care less about gold. I stared at him, Don't be absurd man, of course not, they're dumb animals.

Six months later they filmed the opening of the mine, the excavations a gaping red hole in the earth. The gold was already starting to flow. The company's stock quadrupled, and I was promoted to head office. And the natives have tasted the fruits of their success, droned the narrator's BBC voice, Only a year ago these people were living in tribal poverty but today they enjoy a wealth which is the envy of anyone, all thanks to the Imperial Consolidated Mining Company. We saw a man naked except for his penis horn mowing a lawn by a bungalow. One of his wives was grinning at the camera, wearing nothing more than an apron. The narrator continued, It's a lovely day, and Mrs. Bangalooloo's off to do the shopping, the first supermarkets are on their way.

Up the River

Hidden under ferns in the crippling heat, we'd been watching the group all day through binoculars, Caruthers constantly taking notes. I wondered why because hitherto he'd never show interest in anything other than military history, mining, and fly fishing. Twilight came, and it was time to return to the camp. When he finally gave the signal, we crept away till we found the trail. Well old chap, what do you think? Actually, I replied, It seems to me that their life is a continual orgy. Caruthers smiled, Rather like certain quarters of Port Campbell. Yes, I said, London no different. Chaps putting their most prized possession in the regions of ladies where I wouldn't introduce the stipule of my umbrella. I always wondered who Campbell was, by the way. A strong loined progenitor, Caruthers replied, Dozens of natives entitled to wear Campbell tartan. The story of the Scottish Highlands with an English appendage, he added, Interesting, the comparison. Savage lands, savage lands.

Caruthers chuckled, Oh, in the old days, the biggest challenge was acquiring a wife. Besides the District Commissioner's daughters, there wasn't much to choose from, and they weren't exactly beauties. Young bachelors getting on in the world, and there we were stuck in the furthest corner of the Empire. Illustrious career in the Colonial Office, and nothing for a proper wife. Shackled we were, caged by our success. We'd sit about at sunset nursing our pink gins. For months we had rumors about teachers for the school. The steamer making its journey every two weeks, we'd congregate on the dock watching as it struggled upstream against the current, a white dot growing larger as it progressed against the black of the river. All we were thinking about was some suitable females might be on board.

One day, we got word of some developments during a terrific thunder storm, no-one could hear a thing due to the static. The name Leslie Rogers was all we gleaned. We were on the dock at the appointed hour with our binoculars, making all the right noises, By Jove sir, here she comes, what, another hour or so, steady on steady on, as the dilapidated vessel made its gradual way. Standing in the bows, not the women of our dreams, rather one bald, lean, very tough individual with a countenance like old leather, a Classics master from one of the Great Schools, and we went back to our posts terribly dejected. Well, the poor fellow died very soon after, tick bite fever or some such thing. Awfully nice chap actually, missionary type, very zealous, but not quite what we wanted you know. We buried him and that was that, we made an effort to keep his grave tidy.

Time went by. The usual complaints, the rhythm of the tropics, pink gins, desk work, forays into the hinterland to sort out tribal disputes, staggering heat, then out of the blue the steamer arrived taking us all unawares, and there she stood. Marjorie? I said. Caruthers nodded, Yes, Marjorie, I'll never forget her descending the gangplank, her face, her eyes, hair like an angel, ladylike yet tough, I could see that right away, the school teacher. By gad sir, they muttered. Well, they all made a dash for her tripping over each other, bumbling about, trying to assist her with her luggage, quoting Shakespeare, Ovid, flexing muscles, cracking jokes, twiddling moustaches, whatever they thought might impress her. But I knew I'd won her the moment she stepped down the gangplank. How? I asked. Because I made no moves to assist and she liked that, she was from Cheltenham Ladies, you know, very tough, we were married within the year. I laughed, Women are so odd. Caruthers smiled, An understatement old fellow if I ever heard one, the more I've known the less I understood about them.

Not like those lady chimps, I added. Caruthers offered me a cigarette, Don't you be fooled, they're far cleverer than we imagine, we're just at the beginning, they get jealous too you know. And never forget, they had two Bushmen in the primate section of London Zoo at the beginning of the century until someone mentioned the oddity of it all. Who are we to comment? You know, I agreed, You really have something there. And I've heard, Caruthers interrupted, There's a lovely young thing up country studying chimps, name's Jane something or other, protégée of that Leakey fellow we once met. I wonder what dear old Edgar Rice Burroughs would say, why I'm taking such prodigious notes in my spare time, old chap, hope to liaise with her at some point you know, share some ideas on the subject. Quite, I agreed, Of course, with Marjorie gone, and all that. Exactly old man, said Caruthers, Exactly. Well, here we are, I'll build the fire if you prepare the pot, pour me some of that Glenlivet will you.

The Cutter

There he was again, and it was always the same routine. I watched in the mirror, eating the beef, the frijoles, the tortillas and salsa, while he cut his stomach with the machete. The thin lines in his dark flesh ran with fresh bright blood onto white dungarees. I watched for a long time, interested, my appetite no longer affected because I witnessed this every night. It had been months now. I saw myself in the new customers, how it was the night when first I encountered him. I saw the disbelief, the horror as, looking up from the plates of food, food they were enjoying, good wholesome delicious food, they were confronted by a strange bright eyed bleeding man. Cutting himself with a machete. For money. Or was it something else?

I grinned, sipping my beer. They became pale, tense, trying to ignore him, hoping he would go away, but he never left until they paid. He just cut himself a bit more, waiting. He knew they would eventually succumb. Strong willed, some tried to outlast him. But he always won. The blood flowed, it was all too much. What could you do? Your girlfriend was there, your wife, you were eating your meal, it wasn't supposed to be like that. It was all too much. The coins fell onto the table, angrily rummaged from a pocket. Maybe even a note. Thus he worked his living, restaurant to restaurant, table to table, night after night, in the small provincial town. The waiters pretended he was not there. After all, what can you do with a man like that?

Alarmingly, sometimes the blood ceased to flow. Only plasma, exuding sticky gold like oil. Now and then, when he had been at it for too long. His muscular torso rippling, he tugged and pulled at the lacerations, opening them, cutting more, rubbing the wounds until they bled. His eyes shining. He made a good wage.

Inevitably, he came to my table. He knew me by now. I grinned, pointing. He smiled. I gave him a 200 peso bill, Don't cut yourself for me, my friend. After all, it was a hell of a show, no need to do any more. May God grant you all that you desire, he replied firmly, moving towards the next table. I did not bother to watch. I knew the routine. Observing myself in the mirror, I cut into the beef, adding a little salsa. I savored the taste of the blood, the meat softening in my mouth.

Teams

The jeep blocked our way. A lieutenant jumped out, pointing a pistol. A truck stopped beyond. The crunch of boots on the stones. Indians holding rifles, copper faces passive beneath American helmets. They stared through bloodshot eyes. The lieutenant pushed past, our age, lean, his skin very white in the headlamps. Halt, he shouted, even though there was nowhere to go. I raised my hands. Like a movie. Gazbo did the same. The lieutenant leveled his pistol, pushing it into my face. Turn round, he yelled, his breath reeking of tequila, Now. We faced a low wall. The barrel of a gun pressing between my shoulder blades. My legs kicked apart. Hands frisking thighs, my groin, under the armpits, ribs. Gazbo was shaking.

Who are you? shouted the lieutenant, Turn round. We're students, from England, we're on an exchange at the university, I enunciated. Why are you out this late? What are you doing this late? The lieutenant's voice cutting, without a note of understanding. We've just had dinner, I explained, At the Palace Hotel. You can check with the waiters. I have the receipt in my pocket. Show me, the lieutenant spat, And your papers. Now. Hurry. We emptied our pockets, producing the documents, my meanness our salvation. I only kept the receipt because Gazbo owed me for the meal.

The lieutenant studied the items. Why are you in Mexico, what are you doing in my country? We're here to study Spanish, I said, It's the exchange program of our university. He leered, You already speak Spanish. Why do you need to come here when you already speak Spanish? I shrugged my shoulders, The professors said we needed to improve. The lieutenant calmed down, I was in the Faculty of Law a year ago, then I left, I was wasting my time. Where do you live? I indicated with my raised hand, The Monte Santo building. Gazbo was trembling uncontrollably, his teeth chattering as if he was terribly cold. The lieutenant pointed the gun towards his head, What's wrong with him? Why doesn't he speak? He's ill, I said, He's got a lot of problems, his Spanish is poor. We live across the water, over there, I continued, We were going home.

You are Americans? From New England? No, we're English, England, Liverpool, the north of England, Europe. Liverpool? whispered the lieutenant. Yes, Liverpool. He moved towards me, Liverpool? The same place, I said. The lieutenant lowered his pistol, Magnificent, you like soccer? We're crazy about it, I said, We watch it all the time. We play against locals on the pitches near the jungle. The lieutenant replaced the pistol in his holster, Yes, we play there too, I think I have seen you. He indicated the troops, We are a team, Azteca Militar. The soldiers lowered their weapons. Some of them were grinning, it was obvious they were stoned. Soccer, he shouted suddenly, I have watched Liverpool on television, I love soccer, soccer's my religion. Liverpool is the greatest team. Kevin Keegan, he is a god. He placed his hand on my shoulder, Listen, get home fast, stay off the streets. It's very dangerous. Something happened. Go home, and don't go out again till after dawn. If we see you we will shoot, we won't ask questions, this time you were lucky. We'll go now, I said, It's only two minutes from here, we'll go immediately, that's where we were going. The lieutenant pushed me, Go then, go quickly. He patted Gazbo, returning our documents, ordering the men into the truck before he climbed into the jeep. Kevin Keegan, yelled the lieutenant, Kevin Keegan. I raised my hand, shouting, Kevin Keegan. Gazbo saluted, mumbling, Kevin Keegan. The lieutenant banged his fist on the door. Grinning, he waved. The jeep sped off, followed by the truck. They disappeared into the night, towards the edge of town and the jungle.

Walking over the bridge, we watched until the tail lights vanished. We lit cigarettes. My hands shaking, I inhaled smoke. Gazbo pointed, What the fuck was that about? Fuck knows, I replied, Something happened. This fucking country, he muttered, We've only been here two weeks. Kevin fucking Keegan. Whatever next? Lucky he didn't like Manchester though, eh? Imagine that. Imagine if he fucking supported Manchester. Munich and all that, we'd be fucking dead by now. I nodded, Yeah. It helped we were students, I added, And white.

The caretaker was asleep on the table in the foyer, snoring loudly, his head in a pool of saliva. Someone was smoking marijuana, the odor saturating the corridor. We crept past like burglars. Listen, Gazbo whispered, There. Far away, bursts of gunfire, like firecrackers. The dogs howled for a while. Then silence.

The Game

Check. I had him, my knight attacking his king. My father took a deep breath. Good move son, you're definitely improving. He pondered the situation, Bishop takes knight, you didn't see that did you? You've got to be careful of those bishops. We played on, the oil lamp flickering in the damp breeze, the tropical dark seething with unseen things beyond the verandah. The garden was out of bounds at night, recently the gardener killed two cobras near the compost heap uncovering a nest. I watched a lizard stalking a moth across the ceiling. Home from school for the holidays, and I was beating my father at chess. Wait till they heard next term. I saw myself announcing in no uncertain terms, I played my father at chess, and I won. Then I perceived the opening. If only . . . if only he moved that pawn. He moved the pawn. My queen closed for the kill, the rook supporting, mate in three. Check. He watched me, a faint line of sweat beading his brow, You've been playing a lot? I nodded, In the team, Mr. Robinson's the coach. He grinned, Well, when you see Mr. Robinson next term, you tell him from me that he's been doing a good job, you hear? Yes dad, I replied. In the meantime, he added, Go fix me a pink gin will you? The lizard caught the moth, mashing the dusty meal in its jaws.

I poured the clear liquid into the glass, breathing juniper. Then tonic, finally a touch of Angostura bitters, the drops exploding like blood. Mixing the contents, looking over my shoulder, I took a sip, then another. With his back to me, focused on the game, my father didn't notice. I placed the glass in front of him. He looked up, Thank you son. We resumed play, but the situation had changed. A pawn was blocking my rook. You moved, I said. No, not yet, he replied. But the pawn. What pawn? That pawn wasn't there before, I insisted. Nonsense son, you just don't remember. Frowning, I stared at him. He stared back. The darkness a crescendo of crickets, the occasional screech of a monkey. Knight fork, he said, Watch how the queen works here. It was dangerous but there was a way out because I had more pieces. For a while I blocked, then came the opening. This might be the end, I said advancing my bishop across the board, Check. My father started laughing, Good gracious young man, you could be right, let me think carefully about this one. For a long time no-one spoke. The wind was strengthening, far away a rumbling of thunder. My father looked up, I think there's going to be a storm. Go and make sure the windows are shut, will you? And tell your mother.

I ran through the house closing windows. There's going to be a storm, I shouted when I saw my mother in the bedroom, Dad told me to tell you. I dashed away before she could reply because she would tell me to go to bed and I was going to beat my father at chess. Lightning illuminated the sky revealing big puffy clouds the color of mud. Pulsating shadows danced along the walls. I sat down ready to finish the game. Then I noticed a pawn blocking my bishop. You moved again, I said. I most certainly did not, replied my father. You did, I know you did, my bishop had you in check, and now there's a pawn. Look here, young man, I think you're imagining things. Isn't it time you went to bed? Outraged, the words spilled out of my mouth, You're cheating, I know you are, you're a cheat. Then I realized what I'd said. It wasn't supposed to be like this, and I burst into tears. My mother appeared. What on earth is going on here, she asked, What's all this dreadful noise? Dad's cheating, I yelled before my father could say anything, I was winning and he keeps changing the board. Hands on her hips she glowered at him, Is this true? You ought to be ashamed of yourself Peter, she scolded, Teasing the boy, you're supposed to be teaching him chess. Leaning back in the creaking wicker chair, my father was laughing. Actually, he said gradually regaining control, Actually, the boy's teaching me chess, but I'm teaching him life.

The Garden of Remembrance

The clock struck six. News, screamed my aunt. The BBC pounding through the house. I stood in the doorway, watching the swallows flitting about the eves. Butterflies shimmering through the roses like cellophane, I had never seen so many. I tried to light the cigarette again. I held my arm with the other hand but it was no good. Weeping, I marched to the lobby. The cat stared unblinking as I removed the Pepsi. Giving it the finger, I guzzled the liquid, then I filled the tankard. Your mother's in the garden, my aunt yelled, I don't want to be disturbed, I've got a lot to do for supper so why don't you keep her company.

Putting on sunglasses, I wandered outside. I placed the Pepsi on the grass, pulling a chair over. My mother was sitting in a deck chair nursing a Scotch, Ah, there you are. I won't offer you any, of course. You're drinking cola again, it's so good to see. Charlotte must be relieved. Sit down and let's have a nice chat, it's so nice to have some time at last. The light crackling, I grimaced, my mouth too dry to speak. She stared, Why are you shivering? It's nothing, I replied. Blessing the Russians, I gulped the Pepsi.

Clearing her throat, she commenced, Did I tell you about my trip to South Africa? No, I murmured, You didn't. I drank more Pepsi. The shaking diminished. I lit the cigarette. By the way, you really ought to stop smoking, she sniped. It's really none of your business, I countered. Her jaw tightened, Well, I met some very interesting people in Cape Town, very pleasant. They had a yacht, quite remarkable really, they sailed it from New York. Good Lord, I interjected without interest, Really? Yes, she continued, I met them one evening, we all went out to dinner, in the waterfront you know, where we had dinner with your father that time, before his decline. She sipped demurely, Well it's all changed, must be more than thirty years now, all done quite beautifully, lots of restaurants and cafes, spotless, impossible here of course. You should move, I suggested, Live there during the winter, it would do you the world of good, then you wouldn't complain about the cold and everything else. Why don't you go, why don't you go for a long trip? I've thought about it, she agreed, As you know, but there are so many practicalities, and your aunt isn't getting any younger.

I peered round watching my aunt vigorously washing some lettuce, her stern gaze focused on the sink. Anyway, what was I saying? She sipped the Scotch. Yachts, I prompted, People from New York. Oh yes, well, the wife was very attractive, late twenties, the husband in his fifties, I assumed it was a second marriage or even a third. Maybe a fourth, I mumbled, Or a fifth. My mother frowned, Well, she was wearing a headscarf, very nice, and I commented on it, it was really lovely, I think it was Balinese, I thought of you because you'd been to Bali, she was so attractive. Really? I said not understanding why this obscure meeting should deserve such detail. I finished the tankard. Well, she wore it everywhere, and do you know why? No, I said. My mother took a large sip, She had just had a brain tumor removed. It was her last trip. She had about two months to live. She's dead now. They spread her ashes at sea.

I leaned back in the chair, staring at the sky. I wonder why you have to talk about something like that at this precise moment, I enunciated, Like discussing cadavers at a picnic. My mother glowered, I thought you'd be interested. My hands quivering, I inhaled smoke, fighting to keep my voice steady, Well, I find it very odd that you have to raise the specter of something so awful at this precise time. You know how things have been, with Charlotte's health, it's really very cruel, very insensitive, it's almost as if you're doing it deliberately. I'm having a perfectly good time, she trilled, Aren't you? I remained silent. The sunlight shining rancid butter orange through the trees.

I refilled the tankard, Anyway, let's change the subject, I didn't tell you, Charlotte and I have decided to start a family, we both agreed it might be a solution, something to aim for. Just in case. Life must go on, don't you think? It hasn't been easy for her as you know. My mother drained the Scotch, tossing the ice into a flowerbed. You'll regret it, she said standing up, It's never over, they're with you for life.

The Links

Nice shot, I said. Caruthers peered into the shimmering distance, the turquoise ocean almost metallic under the sun, Not bad, drifting a little to the left, just hope it doesn't bounce into the jungle. Looks good to me, I replied. The glorious seventeenth, he lectured, Often the make or break, always a chance for a hole in one here, for the daring, who dares wins as they say, hope you're insured old man. He chuckled. Watch the breeze, he added, Always a slight breeze off the ocean. I selected a five iron, wiping sweat from my eyes. Late afternoon, the sauna air like a heavy wet towel. Relaxing, I raised the club, following through. Straight down the center of the fairway. Good shot, old man, a good two hundred and fifty yards. The white dot soared, landing, bouncing a few times. I think I'm in a little rough to the left, muttered Caruthers, Didn't quite see where it went. Monkey, him come, said Caruthers' caddie pointing. Damn them, Caruthers cursed.

A troop of ten or so Wadell's monkeys loped onto the course stopping near my ball. A large male picked it up, examining it, then suddenly he threw it away with great ferocity. The troop scattered. A couple of babies ran around, the mother ambling behind. A young male chased them playfully, scooping up the orb. He stared, contemplating, and he began chewing it. Losing interest, he wandered off. There goes another one, I observed. Caruthers was livid, Blast them, here we are, we control the country, but there's nothing we can do about the bloody monkeys. Well, at least I don't drop a shot, I replied. Of course, Caruthers agreed, But if I calculated how many Slazengers I've lost in this fashion, I must have gone some considerable way towards helping the company remain profitable. We strolled after the caddies, who showed no fatigue in the crippling heat.

Caruthers was furthest from the green in some rough. I saw him stumbling in the long grass, hacking at the vegetation in order to scare away snakes. I stood with my caddie, while the furious stocky figure took his stance, no doubt with a seven iron. He sliced into the grass, the shot veering wildly to the right. Oaths and curses wafted on the breeze. Master very angry, said Samson. Yes, I agreed, It was the monkeys. Monkeys very bad sah, very bad. Samson was grinning, enjoying every moment. I smiled. Brodrick, I heard, Brodrick, dammit, where in hell's name did it go, the sun was in my eyes. I too was dazzled. The expanse of the Indian Ocean lay to our right, and I had a sinking feeling that the ball had entered its vastness. I really didn't see old chap, I shouted, Sorry. Caruthers strode towards me, holding his iron like a shotgun, his caddie far behind. If it's any consolation, I said, Look. The monkey had partially eaten the hard coating, rubber bands spewing like guts out of interior.

Frowning, Caruthers puffed on a cigarette, Well, I lose a shot, seeing as the object of my attentions went its merry way unto the depths of Father Neptune, and you are the beneficiary of a local hazard. I selected a new ball, dropping it over my shoulder, as did Caruthers. We played on, both of us reaching the green. I was in for par and, amazingly, Caruthers holed a twenty foot putt for a bogie. Great recovery, I said, Really tip top. He smiled, Lady Luck, old chap, I really didn't know which way it was going.

We teed for the eighteenth, the hole far simpler, just straight, par in four. We both landed on the fairway. Do you remember Joyce Beath? asked Caruthers. Of course, I replied, And her husband Charles, a splendid fellow. Did you know she once killed a woman? No, I replied, wondering how the fourth daughter of The Duke of Argyll might have murdered someone. Caruthers continued, She teed off on the first, right in front of the club house, wonderful shot straight down the center, and at that precise moment a native woman emerged from the trees, hit her square in the temple, killed her stone dead. How awful, I said, What happened? Well, Caruthers continued, There was an arrangement, Joyce paid the deceased's family two hundred pounds thereabouts, a fortune at the time, and the matter was forgotten, just one of those things. I waited while Caruthers concentrated. He swung, achieving an excellent trajectory, landing near the green. Well done, I said. He was grinning, Thanks, amazing what it does to one, sometimes everything hinges on a shot.

Strange how things arrange themselves, I observed. Caruthers laughed, Well, I remember when I was in the Congo before the war. I was playing against Archbishop Guignol, the Primate, and he landed in a rhino print in the middle of the fairway. Well of course, we knew that there were specific rules relating to local challenges of this ilk, and he wouldn't lose a shot, just like you with those blasted monkeys. Still, he was irritated, even if he only needed to chuck the damn thing over his shoulder. For some reason, the monkeys there were never such a problem. I broached to him the relevance of rhino prints at St. Andrew's and how this might relate to the adaptation of the Church, golf rules being a metaphor, and the game ended there. To my surprise, he became rather angry. We went our separate ways. Yet, the more I thought about it, the more significant it became. Really? I quizzed. Caruthers stared, Oh, it was another part of the Empire, but surely you remember Maryville? The massacre? Caruthers nodded, They killed the Mother Superior. Take, eat, this is my body, it was all interpreted a little too literally. Good God, I muttered. That's a matter of perspective, said Caruthers cheerily, Your shot. I hit with all my might, landing on the green. Lovely, he joked, You're up for a birdie. Some sustenance at the nineteenth? Seventh heaven, I yelled. Samson was smiling. Here, I said, handing him a packet of cigarettes and five shillings, For you, I can carry it the rest of the way. Oh, bass, thank you bass. Go on, I said, And say hello to your family. Waving, he ran away.

Ambush

My round lads. I rise and walk towards the bar, your perfect friendly Irishman, the one they sing about in the songs. I'm the enemy no-one knows, a skinny fellow working a construction site, an illiterate Paddy waiting for the next call. London, where you disappear, and I've disappeared all right. Four pints when you're ready, I shout across the smoke. Saturday night, the usual crowd, tourists, yuppies from the City, associated tarts. I've been refused before for being Irish. It was exactly a year ago today, like a birthday.

It all went wrong when me older brother bricked a constable. Mick's his name, doing life. Can't get more Irish than that, eh? Lack of imagination on me parents' part. Me own name's Patrick, believe it or not. RUC the man was, and he died of a brain hemorrhage within the week. So they came for Mick, as I knew they would. The twat already had a record so it was donkey's work to find him. Down comes the door at 5.00 a.m., me Pa trying to stop them till they crack him with a truncheon, Ma screaming like she was going to die. Then Mick squirming out of the window until he got stuck and they battered him. All well and good, I thought, Now we can all go back to bed and get some sleep, the cunt got what he deserved. But they hadn't finished. They started to go through the house destroying it room by room. An official search, said the officer with a Public School accent, Nothing to be afraid of, if we had nothing to hide, just routine.

They found me sister, Oonagh. She was in bed. She's done nothing you bastards, I yelled, but they bust into her room all the same. A squadee punched me back against the wall while another pulled off the bedclothes. Come on then, he said, Show us what you've got. The accent East London. He manipulated the muzzle of his rifle under her knickers and put it into her. There you go, you little slut, how's that then? She made no noise, not even a whimper. He pushed it in further, Come on then, come on, you little slut. The officer came up the stairs, All in order Cummings? He stopped in the doorway when he saw what was going on. Just making a search of some cubby holes here, sir, replied Cummings saluting. The officer began to laugh, Yes, rather, I see what you mean. Come on, we're off, let's get this slab of meat into the wagon. They were hauling Mick down the stairs. Ma was on the sofa drinking a cup of tea, should I say clutching a cup of tea, because if she'd tried to drink she would have drowned. I never told her what happened to Oonagh. They'd taken Pa to the hospital for concussion.

We could have complained. We could have written to the newspapers. We could have contacted our MP. We could have called the police. We could have done a lot of things, but would it have done any good? If you ask around, you'll find what happened to us is normal, everyday, nothing special. Stuff like that is never reported because the people who write the rules write the news. I left school the same day. That was it for me, from now on I was going to write me own fucking rules.

I knew who was in, so I hung about the Falls. Everyone knows who the boys are. Some of them lads me own age. One day, I approached a group in a corner of the pub, the shadows so dark you couldn't see the faces. Sit down, young fella, I heard. A kindly voice. An old man, from the Republic by his accent. What can we do for ye? I told them what happened, I wanted to join. Yer a bit young aren't you m'lad? I mean to say, shouldn't you be in school? No younger than some of them, I said pointing. True m'boy, true, but you'll have to be proving yourself now, dy'hear? Give me a chance, is all, I said, You can check me out, I'm all right, just give me the chance. We will in time, said the old man, You know we will, but we knows you're local, that at least. O'Donohugh's your father is that not correct? That is he, I agreed. The old man drank some beer and sighed, And ye had some trouble with Her Majesty's boys. Well, ye'll hear back from us either way, within the month. Don't you be coming here to see us again now, y'hear.

Six months on a farm in Armagh, living in a cellar, farm work in the day, training at night. Long runs, further every week, tactics, watching from woods, getting to know the land like me own street. Handle a Bren better than me prick. Others arrived. They said the piker organizing us had been in the Foreign Legion, I never knew his name. But he knew his trade. One day, over breakfast, the piker said, Today. We staked out a road, ten miles away. Farm vehicle ready to break down, tall hedges on a corner, one way out, the killing zone. Explosives either side, below a wooded slope for refuge when the deed was done. We waited a day and a night.

The morning of the following day they came, two armored Landrovers crawling along like beetles. Eight squadees and an officer. Very early, just light, the dew thick on the grass. First insects stirring, far off the cooing of a dove. On they came, and the first explosion, then another. Black smoke rising into the mist. Briefly, ever so briefly, I thought, I shouldn't be doing this because I saw a lad me own age running down the lane. Red cropped hair, face white with terror. Then someone shot him down, so I opened up with the Bren cutting open a squadee's chest. I emptied the magazine into the Landrover while the other burned. C'moan we're out of here, shouted the piker, and we were running to the woods. After burying the guns, we went our separate ways. I rode a bicycle to Belfast, and that was that. I never saw them again, and the incident was never reported.

There you are lads. I place the pints on the soaking table. What took you, you silly Irish cunt? says Busby, me Brummie mate. You'll not be using language like that in my presence, I reply, You watch your tongue now ye fucking slag. A pretty girl smiles. I stare at her and she looks again. If you'll excuse me gents, I say, I'm going to seek fairer company, no insult meant Busby m'boy. I flick his ears, stand up, and I walk towards her muttering, Irish bastards for the Kingdom.

The Jungle

We waited for the American outside the shop. It was ten past twelve. Bet he isn't going to show, grumbled Gaz. We'll give it half an hour, I said, Then we'll go. The day was very hot, the sky a deep clear blue. The middle of the day, and we were the only ones in the street. Gaz smoked a cigarette staring into the glass. What do you think about all this? he said. Better not to know, I replied, Useful if we get any trouble though. He nodded, Yeah. Keep on the right side of him for sure. Oh, he's OK, I said, Seems to like us. We're white after all. Gaz started to laugh, smoke belching out of his mouth, White might is right, America, he grinned, Fucking America, seig heil. Hey, you guys, I'm late. The American was strolling up the street in the shade, I got held up. The guy who was supposed to give me this was late. He waved a fat roll of newspaper. You wait till we get into this. Glad you could make it. He was sweating heavily, his purple T shirt soaked through. Don't worry, I said, We've only been here about ten minutes. The American was rummaging with his keys and the lock, You guys all right? I'll roll a couple of cigars, and then we'll get going. Lucky with the weather. How's work? I asked. Oh, quiet, everyone's on holiday. Gonna get busy though, got a visit in a month. Someone coming down from the north. A big shot.

The shop was blissfully cool. You guys sit down, I'll be a couple of minutes. We sat at the table beneath the chandelier, the sweat cooling on our brows. Now get a look at this. He carefully unraveled the newspaper, revealing part of a lush green bush. The quantity and the odor were intimidating. I could tell it was going to be stronger than the stuff the night before. Gaz looked at me and raised his eyebrows. Good, I said. Oh, yes, said the American, This is the mother of all plants. That guy you met last night, the guy with the hands. His father grows this out in the country. Fresh, absolutely fresh. Plants as high as this room. In the hills. He quickly rolled two Havanas, slipping them into a tin which he shoved into his pocket. Then he packed more weed into two old Marlboro cartons.

For you guys. We'll pick it up on the way back. For you to enjoy at your leisure. Should last you a while. I'm leaving again soon so I'll give you some now. In case I don't see you. Thanks, I said. Yeah man, thanks a load, said Gaz. The American grinned, De nada. Vamoos. I can get it any time. He locked the door, and we started walking.

The town had been a Spanish fort, built when they defeated the Aztecs. The old quarter was clustered around a steep hill, the cathedral and the houses constructed from crude blocks of stone. We walked downhill over cobbles through narrow winding streets, the houses becoming shabbier as we reached the outskirts. Cobbles gave way to dirt. Dense vegetation trying to invade the modest space carved out by human beings. When we could see the beginning of the jungle, we were in a shanty town, an illegal settlement. There was no road, just paths between the shacks beaten into the dust by generations of bare feet. The inhabitants were Indians. They stood watching us as if we had just stepped out of a UFO. They're harmless, said the American, They think we're gods.

We crossed the red earth soccer fields, and entered the jungle. For a while, I could still hear the occasional truck, or hammering, a car horn, but these fragile reminders were eventually lost, the only sounds being the crunch of our footfalls on the path, the infrequent shrill call of a bird high up in the treetops. Twilight, impossible to know the time. Where exactly are we going? asked Gaz. It was an obvious question, but we hadn't yet ventured it. The American turned round and grinned, Lambs to the slaughter. Thought you'd never ask. Like I told you, there's an old farm in a clearing, about half an hour from here. We don't want to go too far otherwise we'll have to set off early, to get out before dusk. It's a drag to be here after dark. This guy used to farm duraznos, but he died and the place went to pieces. No-one lives there, and the place is full of trees busting with fruit. You'll see. I come here every year. Usually park the jeep on the other side of the hill and cart the fruit off. I stared at the droplets of sweat dripping from the American's ear. It was hard to imagine a clearing. Hard to imagine anyone wanting to come out here and farm. I wondered how the man had died. Either side of us impenetrable forest, the odor overwhelming, a mixture of new leaves and decay. Clots of fungi. Occasionally the path was lost, but the American knew the route, pushing through the foliage with his arms. I realized why he wanted to be out by sunset. We trudged along in silence, the American out in front, then me, then Gaz because he was tall and had trouble with the branches and vines. The air was stifling, the sweat pouring down us. I would never do this alone, and it was good to see that the American knew what he was doing. I began to wonder about snakes and insects, but I didn't say anything fearing that I would appear foolish. No-one talked because of the effort, and conversation seemed out of place.

Here we are, said the American at last. I could hear a stream, and the air was suddenly cooler. Like entering a cave hacked out of the vegetation. A little grassy meadow, the stream at the bottom of a small hill. The sun penetrated, a sword of dusty golden light. Through the leaves I could see the ruins of a stone farm house. All around, planted at intervals, trees laden with duraznos ready to pick, the fruit ripe yellow. Damn, will you look at that, said the American. Who lived here? asked Gaz. Oh, an old fellow, a Frenchman. Married a local girl back in the '20s, after the Revolution, and he farmed this place till he died. He's buried up there with his wife. The fruit still comes along every year. I always leave some fruit on their graves. The American pulled out the tin. We'll have us a couple of tokes on this, and then we'll get some fruit. Go ahead and start. He handed a lighter and the cigar to Gaz. Concentrating, Gaz carefully lit the end, sucking slowly, inhaling, then once more. Smoke flooded out, momentarily obscuring his head. He passed it to me. Whooooa, he said, as the smoke cleared, God. He seemed to stagger. I drew on the cigar, holding the smoke, then I took another drag. I passed it to the American. I was instantly stoned. The American took three tokes, stubbing out the joint when Gaz and I indicated we'd had enough. Strong? Bloody dynamite, said Gaz, Jesus. See what you mean, I agreed, realizing all of a sudden how much we needed the American. The undergrowth buzzing around me. A pleasant crashing behind the eyes, the air full of life. I didn't know where the hell I was. We couldn't get back on our own. I wondered if Gaz had woken to this. But it was all right. The American wasn't going to disappear. He placed the tin on a stump. I'll leave this with you, if you want any more. I'm going up to get some fruit. I'll bring some back. The American strolled towards the end of the clearing and I watched him vanish over the brow of the hill among the trees. He saw that we were not in a state to walk.

I could barely feel my legs and, when I tried to move, I stumbled. Gaz laughed picking up the tin. It's not funny, I said starting to chuckle, then I was laughing uncontrollably, disturbing the silence. It was like laughing in church. Shhhh, said Gaz. Who's there? I asked. Gaz looked around, You never know. Imagine living here, the Frenchman, at night. Remembering the graves, I shivered, lost, Hey shut it will you. Where's he gone? Gaz stared, Dunno. Jesus. I peered through the trees. Far away I could hear stamping, then shouting, Man this is a bumper crop, I'm coming back here with some buckets. The American was on the hill behind the farm house. Jesus I hope he doesn't fuck off and leave us here, said Gaz. I nodded, Too right. That's some bloody strong stuff, eh? Yeah. We stood in silence listening for something. Just the occasional screech of the bird. Bloody quiet, you'd never think it was this quiet, can you believe it's this quiet? It's not so quiet with you rambling on, I said. He grinned, Silence, the deep silent silence. Think they have leopards here? You what? Leopards, he continued, Leo Pardis, the spotted lion. No way. Then I remembered, Jaguars maybe. Jaguars? Yeah. Unlikely though. But just imagine, I muttered, Just imagine, you're standing here, and then out from the path, a growl, a Jaguar. What would you do? I'd hot-wire it and drive it back to Liverpool, said Gaz. We studied the trees. The vision, a huge striped face leering out of the green. Beautiful and deadly. Last moments, the realization of death. I thought of an old British film. The African night. The horses panicking as something rustles beyond the kraal. The hero coolly saying to his delicate wife, Lion Marjorie, as he loads the .303. I stared at Gaz, Lion Marjorie. He jumped, Hey shut it all right. I don't want to think about it. I can't bloody move, that stuff's got me legs. Me too, I said, Fucking crazy. We stood opposite each other and started to laugh again. Gaz's eyes were swollen and red. Tears running down his face. I could barely stand, my stomach muscles were bunched and I couldn't breathe. Finally I managed to ask, What's so funny? He scratched his face where an insect had bitten him, I was thinking, you know, I'd forgotten, this is the fucking cricket season back home. Can you imagine, I mean what the fuck are we doing here? We're in the middle of the bloody jungle. Somewhere someone is coming in to bowl, the pleasant pock of pig skin on willow, and here we are standing in the bloody jungle. Out of our gourds. And I've got my passport with me and all me papers. Not much use out here, eh? Cricket. Absurdly abstract, the word, the game. Concepts so funny we had to sit down. Shhhh. What? He'll hear. Who? The Frenchman. Shut up. No, the American, he'll think we're nuts. Ah, he's stoned too, said Gaz, He knows all about it, same radio channel. Where the hell is he anyway? We were alone in the silence. Was he watching us? What if he had brought us here to rob us, to kill us. He might be a pathological killer. All the myths about Americans. Crazed Vietnam Veterans. Panic tore into my mind, savaging. We didn't know him. He could be anyone. I looked at Gaz to see if he was on the same band wave, but he was absentmindedly staring at a large leafy plant. A fern. Beneath the plant something moving. A large hirsute creature oozing over the ground through the grass, changing shape as it progressed. I looked closer. A clump of hundreds of hairy caterpillars, clustering together, flowing slowly up the slope. My God do you see that? I whispered. Yeah, said Gaz, Caterpillars, never seen anything like it. You don't want to fall into that. Sting the fuck out of you. We watched the apparition, mesmerized. Hanging together for protection. Like fish in the sea. The ever-present lurking danger within the harmonious beauty. Comfortably forgotten in quiet English suburbs.

You guys wanna come up here? The voice surprised us and we wheeled around as if we had been caught smoking at school. We can't really walk properly, I said. The American was grinning, Told you it was strong. It deserves a word other than strong, said Gaz, Strong is not the word, brain damaging more like. The American clambered down the slope, pushing through the trees. Get a look at these here duraznos. He opened a plastic bag. Have some. We took the fruit, biting into the soft sweet flesh. Juice dribbled down my chin. Bloody good, I said, Just right. I spat some seeds. The American pointed towards the hill, I'm going to come back with the jeep, the old track beyond. Bring a couple of buckets and grab some. They're just here for the birds right now. Going to waste. When did the Frenchman die? asked Gaz. Oh, about thirty years ago. And no-one claimed the land? Nope. Just went back to the jungle. The graves have something to do with it. The locals think the land still belongs to the Frenchman and his wife. Why I always leave some fruit on their graves. Like they're still here. Some Indians live out in a clearing nearby, but apart from them there's nothing for the next two hundred miles. Just the jungle. Then the border and more jungle. And beyond that a war. You come out here much? I asked. Now and then, to get away from it all, bring a joint and get some peace and quiet. Once hiked in a couple of days and camped. Awful spooky though on your own. At night. Never seem to get used to it. Who knows what the fuck's out there. Reminds me of Nam sometimes, 'cept there're no slopes trying to fuck me up. Just a bunch of confused Indians trying to hang onto the old ways. Gotta watch it though, always gotta watch it when you're on your own out here. I was trying to spook him about Jaguars, I said, pointing at Gaz. Bloke's a madman, said Gaz defending himself. Jaguars? No Jaguars here for at least fifty years, said the American, Killed them all off because of the cattle. Nothing out here can do you much harm. A few rattlers, and you gotta watch the coral snakes. They can take you out. Spiders maybe, a few widows around. Some bad plants and fungi. Nothing much. But there's the chupacabras, he added, That's what gets me when I've come out here to camp. Feel like a child all over again, I'm ashamed to say. The chupa what? said Gaz. The American frowned, wiping the sweat off his face, The chupacabras. Something out here kills cattle, especially goats. For some reason goats. No-one knows what it is. No-one's ever seen it. Leaves the goats sucked dry of everything. Just the husk of their skin. Two big puncture marks, and sucked dry inside, no guts left, just the skin. A recent thing. Only been going on for about a year or two. No people as yet though. But they say it's just a matter of time. Holy shit, muttered Gaz. You're not joking? I said. No, absolutely serious, replied the American, Swear to God. Guys have come out here with guns at night to try to kill it, whatever it is. No-one's ever seen anything. Hear stuff though, strange screaming. Happens about once or twice a year. The Indians say it's the Devil. Leaves strange three toed prints, walks on two legs. You're messing us around, I said. No, insisted the American, Really. I mean it. Swear to God. What do you think it is? asked Gaz. No idea. The American paused, Maybe it is the Devil. An eerie silence ensued. Just the monotonous shrill bird call that seemed to originate in my head.

We wandered off, each our separate ways. I wanted to look at the stream to see if I could spot any fish. Gaz was kneeling, examining some mushrooms. The American was standing at the edge of the clearing. He was listening. Something had attracted his attention. I watched him. He turned round and held up his hand. Silence. Then I heard. Hermaaaana. Hermaniiiita. Puuuuto. Far away, muffled, way down the trail, echoing. Gaz stood up. Hermaniiiita, puto gringo, hermaniiiita. Voices carrying through the trees, on the breeze, still far away but growing nearer. Puuuuuto cabrooooon. The American had not moved. Gaz came over. What the fuck's that, he whispered. Someone coming down the trail, I replied, my throat dry with fear, Sounds like several people, not friendly. Hermaaana, hermaniiita. Puuuto griiiingo. Grim calculations already doing their work. The neutral isolation mocking. We could be in serious trouble. It had to be. We had been seen leaving the town. Three gringos, heading into the jungle, beyond the law. Time for revenge. A posse, some local gang. Leather jackets, explosive aggression. Knives. That was the way here, no rules, we were in America, a long way from anywhere. A chance to stomp some whites, spill blood for the humiliations of generations returning with stories of abuse from across the border. We were going to pay for beefy Texans perpetrating hatred on migrants in squalid border jails. No use trying to explain to them, I say old man, wait a minute, actually, you know what, we're not Americans, actually, rather, British you know old chap, we're not responsible, it's really not cricket. Maybe the gringos were carrying money. They knew what we were doing. We were easy meat, out of our heads with marijuana. Just three of us. Ten could take us. Maybe there were more. We were really up the Khyber. I remembered the unique trauma of a fist connecting with my head. The jolting nausea. My brief encounter with university boxing, when I thought I should toughen up a bit, get fit. The controlled environment, a ring with a referee. University boxing when I thought I was tough. That was bad enough, the numbing blows, the blood, the crunching pain of fists hitting nasal cartilage. Here no control, no referee, no Marquis of Queensbury. We were really in for it. At best a severe beating, at worst . . . Hermaaaaana, puto griiingo, yo te chingo hermaniiiiita. The voices nearer. Multiplying. Oblivious to our reactions, the American was quickly working on a large piece of wood, busting it down to form a crude club.

Gaz and I stared at each other, pale with fear. My mouth was so dry, I could barely speak. What do you think's going to happen? I rasped. The dull Liverpudlian accent, resonant with innate traditional violence, Dunno, wait and see. He was a big lad, he had been bricked when he was fifteen. He knew what was coming. Shaking, he started to remove his watch. I followed suit. We were going to make a stand. We had to. There was no choice. There was nowhere to go. The grim logic horrifying. Hermaniiiiiita, puuuuuto griiiingo. Hermaniiiita. Puuuuutooooo. They were close. A couple of minutes, and they would be on us. Maybe twenty of them. I imagined the charging faces filled with blood lust, the smell of violence and sweat. The voices seeming to multiply. There would be a brief exchange of blows, flashing glaring pain, shouts, the loosening of bowels, then a pummeling that might know no end. Our parents receiving news from the efficient clinical consul, They were last seen walking towards the jungle. No traces have been found. We're terribly sorry. A small footnote in the news back home, Students Disappear In Mexico. And everyone thinking, Silly little prats, getting lost in the jungle. Dr. Wright at the beginning of the academic year, And really, no-one has the slightest idea what happened to them. Some might think we did a bunk, and just shacked up with some local women never to return. Pub myths, while our bodies finished rotting in the undergrowth. Maybe some-one would stumble on our bones. We would lie near the Frenchman and his wife. Hermaaaaana. Hermaaaaaniiiita. Puuuuto. The American was jogging towards us holding the club, not a trace of fear, Should've brought a gun, godammit, don't know why I didn't. Fuck it, that would sort it out, the motherfuckers. He pointed, When they come, they'll be out on that path yonder, where we came from. Stick together and fight the hell out of them. Hit them as hard as you can. Really fucking go for them. Show no fear. Sounds like quite a few, but if we make a good stand we might have a chance. A cliché was suddenly real. America, the old logic of the West. Make a circle and fight like hell. Go down fighting. How did we get into this mess? How many hapless fools asked themselves the same question, stuck on the plains while maniac savages closed in for the kill? All those westerns, films about English country lads fighting off Pathans, bayonets, crazed Zulus with assegais, rubbish you watched on a Sunday afternoon with beer, the rain pouring outside, battles you read about, Rorke's Drift, Gordon and the siege of Khartoum, it was about to become our reality except no-one would ever read about it. How we fell under a rain of blows, gloriously beaten to death. I was trembling uncontrollably. Gone quiet, said the American, They'll be coming soon. I could see the strain in his knuckles gripping the wood. We waited, staring at the foliage, silent.

Movement up the path. Positioning maybe, checking us out before the final confrontation. Here they come, said the American. He moved forwards. Gaz and I followed. From my stomach, flowing like sludge through my body into my knees, I felt an embracing weakness. A deadly fatigue. I wanted to lie down and get it over. I wanted to sleep. Stoned. Of all the times to go into a fight. The American slapped the club into his hand, feeling the weight. Just like the old days, he muttered grimly, Takes me back. We'll meet them here. Do as much damage as you can. We were about twenty feet from the path. They would see three gringos, one tanned and hard looking, two pale. They would tell from our eyes who was going to give them the most trouble. We wouldn't last long. We waited. Footsteps, first contact. My heart jolted. The bushes rustled, brown hands pushed the branches aside. A little man walked into the clearing, blinking. Then another, and another. They were about five feet tall, tubby, dressed in jeans, no shirts. They were carrying packages slung beneath a pole. Broad grins revealed bright teeth against their copper skin. Their heads were squat and Asiatic. Indians. I exhaled in relief. Buenas tardes, said the leader. Buenas tardes, we replied. They marched through the clearing back into the jungle. Behind us, as they receded into the undergrowth, we could hear, Hermaaaana, hermaniiita. Puuuto griiingo. Gringo cabroooooon. Exhausted, Gaz sank down onto the turf. I never ever want to experience that again, he said. What the fuck was that all about? I shouted, Fucking crazy bastards. The American was grinning. He had tossed aside the club. Just trying to spook us, he drawled, They knew what we were doing out here. Must've seen us leaving the town. They wanted to fuck our minds. They know what to do. Centuries of experience. Real experts. We'd better get going. We don't want to take any chances. There may be others. And it's going to get dark soon. Remember the chupacabras.

Lions

We docked in Southampton, on April 6th, after a horrendous voyage. I'd been recommended for leave after a bout of fever which had nearly done me in. I didn't want to go but the Governor insisted, Come on old man, he said, It's the only hope, you'll come back right as rain. He meant, after all, that I might not make it otherwise.

I was to spend six months recuperating in England, then I would return to the colony where I was Commissioner for the Ndola region, an area roughly the size of Wales. Colonel Mackenzie had taken over my duties. A thoroughly good chap, very tough.

Owing to the heavy seas, I failed to rest adequately, and my condition worsened. By the time we reached England, I was too ill to stand so they carried me off the ship on a stretcher. Through eyes dimmed by illness and drizzle, I saw my brother and his wife. They hadn't aged a bit. Good to see you Charles, I mumbled, Hello Marjorie. Charles tipped the porters, looming over me, He's ours now Marjorie. Come on Jack, we'll have you up on your feet in no time, nothing good Dorset air can't cure. They loaded me into the Bentley.

I had been away from England for ten years. Ten years in a land either parched or a quagmire of mud. A location so remote there were only six other Europeans in six hundred square miles. Sometimes, I wondered what on earth we were doing there. Ten years quelling tribal feuds, shooting the occasional rabid dog, playing golf, drinking heavily. If you didn't want to catch malaria or sleeping sickness, they said, Drink plenty of gin and tonic. Ten years pampering Chief Lolumgulu and his wives with gifts of umbrellas and silk dresses, and the occasional bottle of single malt scotch whisky. Blended whisky wouldn't do any more. Lolumgulu, without whose approval all the mines would shut down, Lolumgulu without whose welcome we would be dead. I already missed the old rogue.

I'd been pressing the Crown to ban the hunting of Bushmen in South West, it really wasn't on. You had to stay that long to understand. And why, after all the years of success, something went wrong in the mission, and the convent girls ate the Mother Superior. I was the one who found the remains, and shortly after the fevers began. The drums every night till dawn, the occasional roar of lions lounging near the water hole. No doubt that was why I couldn't sleep on the boat. No drums, no lions. I stared through the car window at the emerald countryside speeding past like a film, the beauty like an hallucination. Charles saw that I was awake, You all right back there Jack? Yes, I replied, It's good to be home.

Apparently, I slept for days. I remember being woken every ten minutes by my brother's wife and the maid bringing me soup and water, but later I found out they did this twice a day. Now and then I would see Charles standing in the room. Sometimes I slept so deeply they thought I was dead. I was able to sleep because of the drums. They started every evening at dusk and continued till dawn, a monotonous thudding like a carpet carrying my spirit into the other world, lulling me towards a cure. It was awfully good of Charles to see to it that there were drums, and I wondered who he was employing.

Jolly thoughtful of you to see to it that there are drums, I said one evening when Charles came into the room. Drums? he inquired. Yes, I continued, The drums, without which I wouldn't have a wink of sleep. The main reason I couldn't sleep on the boat. Ten years hearing them in the night, rather need them after all, got rather too used to it, it takes time you know. Which men are you employing? Charles stared at me. Is there something wrong? I added. Nnno, no, not at all, he stammered, Nothing at all, rest Jack, you need to sleep.

So you've been hearing drums? said Dr. Phelan, the Harley Street specialist. Yes, I replied, Can't sleep without them, thought my brother Charles had Africans on the farm. He stared at me for a long time, And I'm told you witnessed something ghastly, quite recently? The Mother Superior, I explained, I found her. Quite, Dr. Phelan interrupted, Quite, I don't need the details, we had a description in the papers several months back. Well, I'm sorry to tell you this, I'm sure you have an idea by now, you're experiencing a complete nervous breakdown, the fevers were totally psychosomatic. If you want your sanity back you'll have to rest. I'm prescribing prolonged rest in hospital, and heavy sedation.

I was not the first member of the family to be done in by Africa. Just over a century before, great great uncle Horatio owned ships running slaves from the West Coast to the Caribbean. Inspired by the codes of the day, he stole vast amounts of jewels from the King of Benin. Told that he would be dead within six months if he didn't return the loot, Horatio pulled out a couple of pistols and shot the King. Horatio returned to Bristol with his gains, and several large parrots. Almost immediately, he began to sicken. Soon he was confined to his bed, nursed by his seven sisters. The doctors were at a loss. He lay in the vast gray room, gradually worsening, mourned over by the women, teaching the parrots obscenities while his life ebbed away. He died at noon, on April 6th, 1825, exactly six months after he had stolen the treasure. Several weeks later, a letter arrived from the West Coast. An old friend and business associate, the writer was worried because the Africans were celebrating Horatio's death with a huge feast. The day of the feast was April 6th, 1825, and the celebrations had started at noon.

As I lay in the sunlit ward, doped to the eyeballs with whatever it was they were giving me, I began to panic. The drums receded over the days and weeks, until I was able to sleep naturally, and now I didn't hear drums at all. Instead, I was hearing lions. Soaked in terror, I told no-one, but the doctors could see that something was wrong because when the lions started roaring around ten o'clock in the morning, and again about four in the afternoon, I shook with fear. Every day I prayed that I would not hear lions, yet every day around the same time, the lions roared. My condition began to worsen. Charles and Marjorie began to visit more frequently, they even rented a flat in Mayfair to be on the spot should anything happen.

He must have got me, I mumbled to Charles one day, I must have done something to anger him, like Uncle Horatio. Horrified, I remembered that I had arrived in England on the same day as my uncle died all those years before. Surely it was more than coincidence. Who? quizzed Charles. Lolumgulu, I explained, It must be Lolumgulu. What on earth are you talking about? Charles shouted. The drums have gone, but it's lions, I murmured, Lions. I'm hearing lions now, lions roaring, always in the morning and again in the afternoon, always the same time. Charles jumped up and started to dance. He ran out of the room. This is it, I thought, It's over for me.

The doctors arrived. Tell him, said Charles. So you're hearing lions, old chap? asked one of the doctors, And at precise times, I'm told? Yes, I replied, Around ten a.m. and four in the afternoon every day, for some time now. I don't know how long I can go on like this. And no drums? continued the other doctor. No, not for a long time now. Wonderful, said doctor number one, You're cured. Cured? I inquired. Cured, he laughed, Totally, utterly, completely cured. You're hearing lions because that's the time they feed the creatures, we're right next to Regent's Zoo you know.

I dressed and left the hospital within the hour. My first duty was to the lions. I gave a check for one hundred guineas to a stunned keeper, with express instructions to buy the finest meat for his lions in token of my gratitude. Then, after cabling the Governor that I was cured and ready for duty, I booked a cabin on the next mail boat to Cape Town. So it's back to Africa, said Charles as we sat in a pub celebrating. Absolutely, old chap, I replied, Absolutely, back to drums and lions.

The Last Supper

We could hear the drums, beyond the walls, the monotonous rhythm like the heartbeat of a vast creature. Every minute, like clockwork, a thudding boom shuddered the building. Dust settled onto the table from the ceiling. Easter, we only had a day to live. Only hours perhaps. They had special ways of killing. A drop more wine old chap? Caruthers leaned across with the bottle, Lots more in the cellar, but we won't have time. Shame really. Thanks, I replied, handing him my glass. He smiled, To the gods old man, to the gods. He lit a cigar, shutting his eyes, and he leaned back in the chair.

We fought our way in after a week traveling through stench, and black clouds of flies feeding on blood. I had never seen anything like it, the massacres, the mutilation. I gazed at the smoldering remains of the town. A ragged figure stumbling towards me across the parade ground saluting in the shimmering heat, Caruthers, Major Caruthers, dashed glad to see you old man, not many of us left you know. I saluted, unable to believe that I was seeing an officer of the Empire. With a bandaged hand, he gestured vaguely at the broken men around him, All officers dead, just these fellows left. He laughed, But by gad sir you showed the devils, what a charge, what a fight, top hole what, you really showed them. They were piling the bodies of the dead, ready to burn, the smell of pitch reminding me of rugby fields. How many men do you have? I asked. Fifty, he replied, Maybe less. Women and children dead. Any chance of reinforcements? I don't know, I said, I sent scouts, when I saw the scale of it. What happened? What in God's name happened? Caruthers began to chuckle, then he began to laugh aloud, as if someone had told a particularly amusing anecdote, In God's name you said, in God's name . . . He was doubled over, whether through pain or laughter I couldn't see. His men were laughing too, low savage laughter, quite out of place under the circumstances. A thin line of blood was trickling down his face, through the bandage around his head. He staggered slightly. The laughter faded away. You ought to rest, I said. He leaned against me supporting himself on my shoulder, I'll tell all old man, he murmured regaining control, I'll tell all. Hear? It seems to be quieter. Come on, I'm sure you could eat. A drop of wine'll put us right, old boy. The smell of the burning bodies had begun to spread, but to my surprise I found I was hungry.

The rebels returned later that night. Now they were ramming the gates using a contraption invented by the Romans. The candle fluttered, the frost signaling the beginning of winter. The stars shone unnaturally bright, and I could see the Southern Cross. Caruthers cut into the bread, Sorry we've nothing else to eat, old chap. I couldn't eat much, I admitted, Damned good wine though. Splendid, agreed Caruthers. So what happened? I ventured, What went wrong? The colony was really prospering. Caruthers stared at me, one eye twitching, It was the monkeys old boy, the monkeys. The monkeys? I asked thinking that he had lost his mind. Caruthers cleared his throat, Yes. The monkeys. We sat in silence as I waited for him to continue his strange explanation. He drank some wine and resumed, And the Bishop. You know who our Bishop was, don't you? Yes, I replied recalling a name, Bishop Stanforth wasn't it? Caruthers smiled, Exactly, Stanforth. Bishop John Stanforth. A fine fellow really, even if he was a pompous ass. I interrupted, I even met him once, I believe, in Cairo, briefly, about five years ago. That's the man, agreed Caruthers, He used to be in Cairo. Before that he was Bishop of Rangoon. Well, he was a funny chap really. Used to feed the monkeys every morning and every evening, on his walk to and from the Palace, twice a day, like clockwork, without fail. Seemed to regard the monkeys as part of his congregation almost. Really an odd chap, most odd. No-one paid much attention. The natives liked him. And the monkeys, the monkeys seemed to love him. They waited for him, dozens of them, they even seemed to know the time. It was all rather a lark. Went on for a couple of years. Malicious tongues used to say they were his most faithful followers. He even joked how he wished his flock were of the same caliber. I chuckled. Caruthers stared at me, his eyes bright yellow in the dim light, Well one day, he forgot to bring food in the evening.

He didn't think anything of it, obviously, because he set off as usual across the park. And the monkeys, well, they tore him to pieces. Good God, I said, still not understanding the connection with the rebellion. Yes, Caruthers mumbled, There was not much of him left. Poor old Stanforth, absolutely torn to pieces. So of course the Governor saw to it that they killed the monkeys. Poisoned them. Every single one. I was very against it, for obvious reasons, I'm sure you understand. Yes, I said, I'm beginning to understand now. Caruthers interrupted, You see, the monkeys had been there for centuries, generation after generation. Look at the carvings on the local temples. It's obvious. Even though they go to church, the natives still worship them. The monkeys are icons, connected to the Great Creator and all that, I'm sure you know. Which was one reason why the Bishop was so popular. He fed them, and the natives loved him for it. Funny, really, isn't it? And something prophesied in one of their books that when the monkeys all die it's the end of the world. So when the monkeys were poisoned . . . Of course, I said, Of course, and it's been like this ever since? Caruthers nodded gravely, Yes. Then there's not much hope is there? I muttered. No, said Caruthers, Very little.

A huge jolt shook the building, covering us with dust. Caruthers stood up, My God, they've blown the gates. A vast cheer drowning the muskets, as hundreds of rebels poured into the fort, the noise merging into the single furious roar of a great beast. Caruthers stumbled towards a shelf. Here, take this, it's better that way. He pushed a decanter of dark red liquid towards me, Laudanum, you won't know anything. Drink it, hurry. Hesitating, I started to fill my glass. Strange isn't it, I said suddenly realizing, Ending like this. With bread and wine, have you thought? And Easter. Shaking, Caruthers turned, and he started to shout, More bloody mumbo jumbo just like the monkeys. And look where it's got us. If only we could all do without it, if only we could just get on without it. He raised the laudanum and was about to drink. Wait, I said, Please wait, you . . . For what, he interrupted, The Second Coming? A brief shout of laughter, and he tipped the cup, swallowing the contents.

Seek and Ye Shall Find

Caruthers, I said to my wife, pointing at the newspaper, They found his skeleton. My God, she replied, Where? In the Arakan, I muttered, Loggers clearing a way through the jungle for a road. She handed me a glass of Glenlivet. And still no sign of the Chimera, I added, They mentioned that. I sipped the whisky, contemplating the years, my memory drifting back half a century. I remembered how we tried to penetrate the country, put our names on things, own it. We'd beaten the Japs, we were there before the Americans. Then we left, and now a Harvard educated dictator was running the show.

The messenger arrived with news. Evidence that Caruthers was perhaps still out there. It was late, a couple of hours till sunset. I ate the rice porridge, then I lay in the hammock under the mosquito netting, smoking a pipe, listening to the porters singing each other stories. I recalled our last meeting six months before, a hundred miles down river. The lean figure, blue hypnotic eyes bright with energy. Brodrick, old boy, he insisted, I've got to go, no choice in the matter. The chance of a lifetime, you'd do the same.

I tried to dissuade him. He was proposing to hack his way into unexplored jungle in search of a plant. A few days earlier, with great ceremony, a tiger hunter presented an unidentified leaf Caruthers believed belonged to the legendary Chimera Orchid. The powder was said to be a powerful aphrodisiac, with the ability to heal wounds and prolong life. Since the war, five botanists disappeared in the region trying to find it. Some pharmaceutical companies were interested.

Drunk on banana gin, the hunter rambled on, lisping between broken teeth. He swore he could find the location. If it isn't the Chimera, Caruthers shouted, packing his gear into the boat, At least I'll have my name on a new species. His parting words, as he set off up river towards the Arakan. He waved, gaunt, unshaven. The little lion medallion around his neck shone in the sun, a gift from a priest in 1943. We served in the Chindits, the war interrupting our careers.

News of his progress became sporadic. Traders talked of the Crudhurs, a giant man who glowed like the moon, he married a chief's daughter, he had found the Chimera, he lived with the gods in the Arakan. Then nothing. Six months, no news. I assumed he was dead, even though he knew the jungle well. I mourned the loss of my friend.

We set off at dawn. The sun barely penetrating the jungle canopy all day. Silence, the occasional screech of a monkey, the splash of something large sliding into the river. Sitting in the canoe while the porters paddled, sliding over the greasy black water, I contemplated the day I saw the Blue Virgin. You've done it, old man, you've done it, Caruthers had shouted, We must celebrate. The Blue Virgin, Lepidopter Brodricki, I searched for two years. My name on a species. With shaking hands, he opened the Glenlivet purchased months before in Umthalang. Reminds me of the Spey, he muttered, The whisky, long for it sometimes, a spot of salmon fishing, Scotland. He wiped the sweat from his eyes. Have you ever thought, I began, The Blue Virgin? Yes, he agreed, Very odd, the parallels.

The natives called the huge blue butterfly Tarang Ma. In Natalangan, the local dialect, tarang meant blue, ma signifying girl, maiden, or virgin. The butterfly laid its eggs in dung, the larva hatching after a few days. For a week or so, before it died, the butterfly flapped about the undergrowth, pollinating jasmine. The grubs contained a substance that, when consumed, induced hallucinations lasting several hours. According to the natives, one encountered Tarang Ma, the goddess of mercy. Caruthers and I experimented and, we agreed, through our dreams we communed with a lithe blue girl of tremendous beauty. I awoke, experiencing misery akin to leaving my mother to start boarding school, when I was very young. The natives claimed that ingestion of the grub enabled the girl to exist within one, bringing protection. One reason why Caruthers and I were able to travel freely in the region. Randomly, the grubs were very toxic. Caruthers and I survived. We had power. Everything was meant to be.

When I finally captured my first specimen, I realized the real significance. Besides the unearthly sky blue beauty of the creature, the colors altering with the light, on the back of the wings I perceived the shape of a woman. I caught several others, finding the pattern to be consistent. Do you see what I see, I asked, Or is it just me? Of course I see what you see, muttered Caruthers, It's almost impossible to believe, and something so lovely emerging from dung. Dung, the dreams of men, he added, There, perhaps, is the connection. Two weeks later he set off on his quest, and I never saw him again.

Eventually, we abandoned the canoe. Rapids, a current impossible to negotiate. We were in the foothills of the Arakan, the vast range towering beyond like a grey tidal wave. After two days, we reached a clearing. Narang territory. The headman was summoned. Children screaming and laughing, women averting their eyes through modesty even though they were naked. I have come for the Crudhurs, I enunciated, I seek to meet with him. Inside the Big House, surrounded by skulls, we smoked jum, the odor like mowed grass. The huge pipe did the rounds, everybody laughing. A good sign because the Narang were headhunters. And I had communed with the Blue Virgin, I was welcome, completely safe.

Apparently, impatient with the guide, out of his mind with fever, Caruthers set off alone. I received his battered leather satchel, the initials HC engraved in faded gold lettering. Inside it, his journal. I leafed through the damp pages, skimming dates, observations, sketches, his unmistakable handwriting deteriorating. The last entry was blurred, the letters spidery.

> What I am seeking may kill me. Yet I would not exist if I had not tried. The tracks I left are gone, there is no path ahead. The clearing in which I lie will disappear.

I imagined the lean figure hacking his way through the undergrowth, stripped to the waist, dripping sweat, his hard body like a peeled tree. One day, decades later, in the depths of the forest, they would encounter the skeleton clutching a machete. A little medallion around the vertebrae.

That night, I lay in my hammock. Disoriented from the march, the jum, the tremendous heat, for want of anything better to do, I opened my Bible. By chance, it seemed, I stumbled on Mathew 7:7, Seek, and ye shall find. Despite the circumstances, sitting in my armchair fifty years later, I found myself chuckling at the recollection.

The Politician

He was a politician, they said, a friend of the Governor, and a few weeks earlier he tried to shoot a priest. He tried to shoot the priest because he said priests were the enemies of the Revolution, and as a politician it was his duty to make sure the Revolution continued its progress. So he tried to kill the priest. He fired six times, but he missed. He couldn't understand how he managed to miss at that range. And then they jumped on him before he got a chance to reload. The people. They beat him up and they were going to lynch him, but he was rescued by the police before they could string him up. It was a bad sign. The people no longer believed in the Revolution when they started defending the priests again. He'd exhorted them to think again, to leave him alone, even to help him kill the priest, then someone hit him from behind and the next thing he knew he was in the police car. It was a very bad sign. Times were bad. What was it coming to? The Revolution. Very bad. He took a long swallow from the mug of tequila, and another. Then he lay back in the armchair, loosened his tie, and fell asleep.

We could hear his snores in the corridor where we were talking to Manuel about bringing the weed. We arrived at the appointed time, as Manuel instructed, and now Manuel kept looking back towards the living room where the politician was sleeping. We've got to be careful with the politician there, he said, If he sees you you're in trouble. But he's out for the count, said Pestañas, It's all right, can't you see? Manuel frowned, OK, come on then. You can try some but I warned you. He can be a sonofabitch, and he hates gringos. It's all right, it's all right, insisted Pestañas, Come on.

We entered the room. It was spacious and cool. Books lined the shelves, and there was a large record collection. A couple of pictures on the wall with random lines and color. Some statement that made sense in the 1920s. Manuel rolled a cigar, and he lit it. He took a few quick drags, coughing, passing it to Pestañas. Pestañas offered it after a couple of tokes. It was very strong, and we were stoned almost immediately. We'll take it, I said, As much as you've got. 1500 pesos? Pestañas asked. I nodded, Sure, whatever, it's good stuff. Oaxacan, said Pestañas, Very fresh. The agreement concluded, we sat back, finishing the joint.

The politician was still asleep, although he occasionally stirred. His tie was lopsided and his dark suit was crumpled and stained. He had greased his hair, but now it was lank and disheveled, hanging over his eyes. Saliva dribbled down his chin onto his collar. Manuel stared, Ever since the priest, he's been like this, drunk all day and all night. I don't know what's happened to him. Guy's fucking crazy, said Pestañas, Fucking out of his mind. Manuel laughed. He pointed at the ceiling, You see those holes? I looked up. There were two large dents like elephant's footprints, where chunks of plaster had fallen away. The rest of the ceiling unblemished. Yes, I replied. The politician did that. How? I asked. Manuel grinned, He tried to shoot himself last year. Twice. He missed once and the second time he just grazed his head. He had to wear a huge bandage for ages. The guy couldn't hit an office block at point blank. Fucking crazy bastard. Why'd he do it? I asked. Manuel gestured to the room, This apartment, it's haunted. We're going to move as soon as we can. I hate this place. It affected him. Even I get depressed here. There's a ghost. He motioned to the politician slumped in the armchair.

I noticed the empty bottle at his feet. He doesn't smoke weed? Oh, he smokes all right, said Manuel, He just doesn't like gringos. He'll bust you if he can. The man's a shit. But he's got connections. That's the only way he gets by. The Governor owes him. For what? Manuel shrugged his shoulders, No-one knows. He's a sonofabitch, said Pestañas lighting a cigarette, I hate his guts. Manuel was rolling another cigar, Here, you'd better take it now, before he wakes, OK. I reached over the table for the bag. At that precise moment, the politician woke up. He frowned, scrutinizing me with a bloodshot eye. What's this fucking gringo doing here? he growled, coughing violently. Phlegm bubbled in his throat. He sat up slowly, looking around dazed. Manuel had lit the joint and he was handing it to Pestañas. I'll bust your sorry gringo ass, continued the politician glaring at me, reaching for a cigarette in his jacket pocket, his eyes unnaturally bright, You'll see. I'll get you. Manuel grinned, He's drunk, he doesn't mean it. Pestañas was silent. I mean it, you sonofabitch, I'll get the gringo bastards. The politician rose and staggered to the toilet. We could hear him retching and coughing. You'd better get out of here now, said Manuel, He'll forget, don't worry. He'll get drunk again, and he'll forget. But you'd better get going. Yes, I said standing up, Thanks for everything. I handed him the 1500 pesos. In the corridor, I could hear the politician throwing up. It's a pity the bastard can't shoot straighter, said Pestañas, The sonofabitch. What kind of guy can't even shoot himself?

The Reunion

Name's McIntyre, Angus McIntyre. It's a pleasure. Last time I tried telling anyone, they laughed, said I should see a shrink. Claimed I'd had too much of the water of life, Usquebaugh, whisky to you. They don't know anything though. Went back to Scotland y'see, with the wife, finally saw the mystery. Got a lot of family there, family I never knew until . . . Well, that's part of the story. Don't want to jump the gun now, do I?

It starts with Grandfather Hamish. Born in Oban, on the west coast of Scotland, he was a merchant seaman until he met my grandmother who was from San Francisco. They married, settled near Sacramento, and he found a job selling insurance. Apart from World War Two, when he served in the Navy, they never left. He prospered and they had a family. The only thing that bothered him was he never went back to Scotland. As a result, he talked incessantly on the subject, especially after a couple of drams, an endless array of anecdotes, some believable some less so. Anyone who came into his orbit heard stories of the Auld Country, how the Chief of Clan McIntyre was alive and well living in upstate New York, he wasn't recognized by the Windsors because he refused to pay the dues, the temporary Chief was a usurper, and Glen Noe should be reclaimed for the Clan. We heard about Cruachan, the magic mountain upon whose summit there is always snow, the standing stones of Strontoiller which occasionally speak when questioned about matters of love and death, tales of poaching salmon and oysters from The MacDougall's territory.

When the wind hurled rain against the sides of the old house in the country north of the city, with the aroma of whisky and pipe smoke, the soft skirl of bagpipes on the record player, it was easy for my father, and later me, to believe that we were not in Northern California but on the Scottish west coast in the teeth of a gale. If only I could get back there, my grandfather used to say, There's one thing I have to do, a man I have to meet, Jock MacKinnon, just for old times, he owes me for something. I always wondered what this debt could be but I never pursued the matter for fear of uncovering some dark deed. But as grandfather always laughed when mentioning the name Jock MacKinnon, I guessed it couldn't be so bad.

The years went by. My father grew up, went to college, qualified as a lawyer, and started a family. I was born, I went to college, qualified as a lawyer, and started a family. Grandfather saw the fruits of his effort, and he died a happy man. We buried him in the family plot alongside his wife under a Celtic cross. But I always felt sad he never made it back to Scotland. Neither had my father, yet we continued the traditions of the McIntyres, telling our offspring the legends, starting with the one about the founder in the 12th century, the strong loined progenitor, who'd cut off his thumb to plug a leak in MacDonald of Sleat's galley, thereby saving the Lord of the Isles' life. In gratitude, the Chief granted him the right to found his own clan. As this long distant ancestor was a carpenter, his offspring became known as children of the carpenter, Mac-an-t-saoir in Gaelic, MacIntyre in English. Per Ardua was the motto, Through Difficulty. We'd done that OK. From being a penniless seaman, my grandfather had founded a dynasty.

With my sons through college, I eased up a little. Then one day I looked at my bank balances, my investments, and I realized I didn't need to work. Oh sure, I'd miss it if I didn't but I could always come back if I wanted, three days a week maybe, and anyway it was time for some younger blood to move up in the company. I talked to Brad Holland, a colleague since the beginning, and I told him I was going to take some time off, I didn't know how long. I was going to visit Scotland, the first member of my family to do so since Grandfather Hamish left in the 1930s. Mac, he agreed, Go for it buddy, you deserve it, when you want to come back we can always use you. Brad was always a hell of a guy. Well, you've always wanted to go, said my wife, Am I invited? If you behave yourself, I replied, You're representing the Clan now, you hear.

Beyond the Falls of Brora, Loch Etive stretches into the misty distance, the vast presence of Cruachan marking the barrier between the Pass of Brander and Glen Noe, the old Clan lands. My eyes watering with emotion, I passed the binoculars to my wife. Can you believe that? I muttered. It's awesome, she agreed. The small launch bobbed on the gentle swell coming in from the sea. To the west great clouds massed against the sky, stained blood red by the setting sun. We'd best be making for home, said Mr. Clark, the skipper, Night coming down. A renowned local deerstalker, Mr. Clark also owned the B and B where we were staying. Sure, I agreed. He turned the wheel, and we chugged down the loch towards Oban, the first stars glimmering in the eastern sky.

We docked. Where would you recommend for a quiet drink and a meal? I inquired. You'd be best trying the Caledonian Hotel, Mr. Clark replied, Ay, the Caledonian, it's a fine place. He tied the boat up and we bade him farewell. Walking along the quay in the twilight, the cry of the seagulls, the steady westerly breeze with its mixture of sea and seaweed. The view to Mull like a scene from legend. Early September. The days were still long, the weather fair, and there were few tourists. Isn't it wonderful, said my wife, I can hardly believe it. I looked at my watch, At this precise time, it's mid-day in SF, eight hours difference. I guess it is, my wife agreed. I thought of the speed, technology, palm pilots, cell phones, SUVs, fast food, caffeine. Refreshing to know the whole world was not that way, there were still places, a different pace, different culture. Sometimes you could never imagine. She took my arm, And we've got all the time in the world, she added.

Back at the B and B my wife wanted to have a bath before dinner. I decided to stroll down to the Caledonian Hotel to see what it was like, and have a drink, and see whether it was suitable. I remembered a big Victorian building overlooking the port. We agreed to meet in about an hour. The town being so small it was a five minute walk. I pushed open the doors and entered an ornate bar decorated with fading mirrors and Edwardian furniture. This would do, my wife was going to love this. Apart from an old man dressed in black with a long white beard I was the only customer. Half of beer, and a shot of MacPhail's, I said to the barman. I had seen the locals drinking this way, Half and a Half they called it. I drained the beer, sipped the shot, and ordered another round, the two drinks complementing each other perfectly. Well, Angus my boy, you look very much like him. I turned. The old man had spoken. He was grinning broadly. His teeth were yellow, like old ivory. Excuse me? I said. Your grandfather, now, don't you be fooling about, you're Hamish's blood and no mistake.

Now, it is just possible that I could be recognized as Hamish McIntyre's grandson through certain family traits, especially to one who knew the old boy well. It is said that a McIntyre can be recognized by the knees, for example, and I had certainly inherited Grandfather Hamish's large ears, and his strong spade like jaw. But Grandfather Hamish had not set foot in Oban since 1933, and anyway how did this old man know my name? I drank some beer, You know my name. Of course boy, of course, replied the old man. How? It was the obvious question. But he just winked and took another sip of his whisky. Then I understood. My father had set this up, or some relative, they had seen to it. Dad was in his seventies but it was just the kind of thing he'd do. I laughed, Here let me buy you a round. No need, said the old fellow, I'm not going to be here for long. By his clothes, I assumed he'd been at a funeral or some kind of memorial, he must be tired. Now the next lad to come through those doors is going to be your cousin Aleister, continued the old man, Should be here any minute. Did you tell him I'd be here? I asked. The old man nodded, In a way yes.

A strong looking man about my age came into the bar. He appeared not to have seen us. The old man chuckled, Go over to him and say, Aleister lad, how are you? Go on now, he'll be tickled. I drained my whisky, walked over, and said boldly, Aleister, how are you lad? Good to see you after all these years. I extended my hand. I could hear the old man laughing. The man looked at me as if I was mad. And who might you be? he asked. I couldn't resist, the situation was too funny. I slapped his shoulder, Angus, I'm your cousin Angus, from California. The man's eyes widened, Hamish's grandson? Himself. Good God man, what're you doing here, how did you know? I winked, not wanting to ruin the fun. The old man was laughing softly. Aleister placed his drinks on the counter. This is special, he shouted, This is incredible, ah cannae believe this, ah've got to get some others. You've got time now? Yes, I replied, All the time in the world, my wife should be here before long. Oh this is magic, said Aleister, Ah cannae believe this. I'll be a jiffy. He dashed out of the bar.

I went back to the old man. You're going to meet your relatives, he whispered, The area's full of them. What an amazing surprise, I said, I could never have foreseen this. The old dog, he's always doing things like this, I added, thinking of my father, not wanting to ruin the aura of mystery unfolding around us. It was like Brigadoon, Brigadoon, except it was really taking place. Several people came into the bar, Aleister, three men, and two women. Aleister motioned, My brothers, Neil, Jock, and Donald, my wife Morag and Jock's wife Katherine. We ordered beer and whisky as more people arrived. Hey, here he is, yelled Aleister pointing at me, Ah cannae believe this. People introducing each other, Duncan, Kinnon, Fergus, Douglas, George, their wives, Moira, Kirsty, Deirdre, Margaret, Iona, cousins, others, younger members of the family, nephews, nieces, an array of Gaelic names like music. I just wish the rest of my family could be here to witness this, I kept saying, listening to complex explanations of obscure family history, And of course Grandfather Hamish. Cousin Doddie leaning towards me reeking whisky, rambling in deep brogue, And it was when Mary married Wylie, that your uncle Tavish left for New Zealand, and me nodding trying to take the whole thing in because it seemed to be getting out of control. More people arrived, and someone with an accordion. Unable to cope, the barman called for reinforcements and now there were three barmen, and even one of the barmen was apparently related to Grandfather Hamish. I waved at the old man. He waved back.

I had to tell my father what was going on, and thank him for setting everything up, the reunion, it must have been him. It was mid-afternoon in Sacramento. I slipped out of the room and the din into the quiet of the lobby. The line was clear after I dialed. Dad, you old rogue, you should have told me. Told you what my boy? Where are you son? Oban, I replied, With a bar full of family, McIntyres, dad, dozens of relatives, people who know you, people who know me, some even knew Grandfather Hamish. You should have told me, it was quite a surprise. He was shouting down the line, What on earth are you talking about, son, have you lost your mind? I persisted, I met an old man, then a cousin came in the bar, the old man knew it was going to happen, you're messing me around here. My father was laughing, Talk some sense son, you're a lawyer aren't you? How much whisky have you had? I countered, You mean to tell me all this was coincidence? There's a bar full of relatives here, and an old man who knew who I was, someone I've never seen before. What's his name? asked my father. I realized I hadn't found out the old man's name, I don't know. So you're telling me you had no part in this? My father laughed, Son, how could I? I don't know anyone in Oban, never been there after all, don't know anyone in Scotland for that matter but I'm glad you're having a good time. OK, dad, I replied, baffled, the mystery deepening, You swear? There's no way I could have set up a meeting, he insisted, How could I? I interrupted, And no-one else, no relatives? Who? he continued, You know, there's no-one who could've done it, not here anyway. You get back to the party, don't think about these things too much, there'll be an explanation somewhere, you know what old Hamish was always saying. There's some strange things happen now and then.

When I returned to the bar, I looked around for the old man but he had left. Then my wife came in. She struggled through the crowd towards me. What on earth is going on? she asked. Then, You're drunk Angus, you ought to be ashamed. They, I slurred pointing, They're all family, McIntyres, would you believe? She peered around the room through the smoke. All of them? she shouted above the din. All of them, I yelled, All McIntyres. How? I don't know, I replied, I thought Dad set something up, but I just called him and he swears he didn't. Your father? Yes. But he's never been here, she laughed, How could he? There was no more room for analysis because then I was introducing her to everyone, and she was being plied with beer and whisky.

For a couple of hours the gathering expanded, spilling into the street around the port, people arriving in cars and vans from the countryside. But all good things come to an end, there is just so much beer and whisky even the strongest among us can take. Thus it was the chief barman observed that it was time to go home, time to shut the bar, even though some were calling for events to continue beyond normal hours, a custom popular in the long dark winters. Only if you all pipe down, boomed the barman, Otherwise we'll be having the whole Glasgow Constabulary onto us, and no mistake.

Towards dawn, when my wife had fallen asleep in one of the big armchairs alongside about fifty other people, cousin Aleister and I were exchanging stories supping a last nightcap. Ah still cannae believe this happened, he said, How on earth did you know I was your cousin in the first place? Well, I explained, You remember the old man sitting in the bar when you arrived, he told me. What old man? I saw no-one except you. The old man, I repeated, He knew Grandfather Hamish, said I looked like him, said the blood runs deep, and it's unmistakable. He told me you were coming into the bar. Good God, said Aleister, I saw nobody, but what did this fellow look like? I mentioned the dark clothes, the gaunt face, the long white beard. Aleister stared at me, his eyes shining, That's old Jock MacKinnon you're describing, he's been dead these last ten years, knew Hamish well. They worked on a boat before Hamish left. Hamish saved his life one night when they went overboard, they were thought to be long dead, but Hamish made it ashore to Kerrera with Jock MacKinnon half alive. The old boy always felt he owed your grandfather, never knew how to repay him with Hamish in America and all that. Well, I muttered, emotion welling up in me as I remembered, I guess he just repaid the debt. He brought us all together.

Sunday Breakfast

We're sitting in the cafe, the main one where everyone goes. We've got our big glasses of coffee, and I'm eating eggs and tortillas, and some jalapeños. The American's there, smoking a cigarette, and Gaz, and two women the American knows. He's going on in English so they can't understand, about how he likes their papayas, their melons, and everybody's laughing, the girls too even though they can't understand. They're big, sure, big round breasts just like fruit, and I'm glancing at them. The girls know, and they catch me, and I look sheepish, but we all laugh. They don't mind. Then we're not saying much, the food's too good. I suck on my cigarette and eat some more of the eggs. I take a mouthful of the coffee, the wonderful coffee they make, knowing it grows in the area, just outside of the town. You can see it wild where it's escaped from the plantations. Everything's quiet and peaceful, and we're thinking, it's Sunday, and how good it all is. Just then there's a lot of noise outside. People are running down the street because something's happened. The American grins, stubbing out his cigarette. He wanders away. We don't pay any attention. I'm finishing my eggs, and Gaz is rambling on about bulls, and regulations to do with exporting bull semen across the frontier. The girls are giggling, and I'm still looking at their fruit.

The American returns, They've just shot the priest. What? we all say at once. No way, I say. Yeah, he says, Someone got up in the middle of the sermon with a gun and shot the priest. Well, that's the funniest thing I've ever heard, and I can't eat any more because I'm laughing so much. And the girls are laughing too but they're concerned, they're saying, Poor little priest, how could they do that to the poor little priest? Is he dead? I ask finally. The American looks disgusted, No, the guy missed, six shots point blank range and he missed. Outside the cafe, a crowd of people are walking down the street yelling, beating up this one guy, the guy who tried to shoot the priest. He's in a suit but he's bloody, and his suit is crumpled and torn. He's shouting something but it's unintelligible. A big peasant knocks him down from behind. Someone says they're going to lynch him, but the police arrive and start pushing the crowd around with their sticks. They lift the guy up and bundle him into a police car.

Why'd he do it? I ask. Why does anyone do anything? replied the American, and Gaz just mumbles, Pity they don't do it more bloody often. Then everyone starts to calm down. I start to eat my eggs again but they're cold by now, so I go back to watching the girls' fruit, and I light another cigarette. Then the American gets up and says he's got to go. The girls follow him and they all file out of the cafe. I watch them as they leave, the heavy ripe thighs of the girls, a little overweight but nice. Nice and ripe. And I'm thinking, It's a pity they had to go so soon.

Sniper

Sergeant Virkov sat in the front of the truck. Legionnaire Stacy drove. In the back, I sat with Donnell, Jrovnic, and Clothard. No-one spoke, partly because of the noise of the engine. The barracks receded into the distance as we sped through the city, then the outskirts. Two police cars joined us as we reached the countryside, the ragged Midi, baking dry in the summer heat. Sweat rolled down my brow into my eyes. I squinted against the glare. Jrovnic grinned, Hot? I smiled. He gestured at the police cars behind us. Jrovnic, with his experience in Bosnia. Why can't they do it themselves, fucking amateurs? Fucking cops. What're they for? We ought to take them out. It was once my pleasure. Save your energy, I said, Don't bother. We'll get this done and go home to dinner. Jrovnic laughed, Domestic. So domestic. I ought to make you my wife. I did not bother to comment. Clothard and Donnell stared at nothing, hearing nothing, as always. They hardly ever spoke. Only God knew where they came from. They were someone's sons, years ago, somewhere. Hard to imagine them as kids, running around at school laughing. Jrovnic lit a cigarette, smoking in silence, staring at the cops in the car behind us. Ash settled on his dark green fatigues before blowing away. Behind the windshield, two beefy faces stared back.

Sergeant Virkov found us before lunch. He said we were going for a picnic. With rifles. The rifles had telescopic sights. We carried live ammunition. An exercise, we thought, An exercise. But by the truck he told us what was going on. Some creep had taken tourists hostage, in the countryside, about ten miles outside Marseilles. We would sort it out. Why can't the cops do it? Jrovnic asked, That's what they're paid for. Because they asked us to do it, Sergeant Virkov answered, And they're incapable, you know that. What about my lunch? continued Jrovnic. Sergeant Virkov ignored him, and Jrovnic knew better than to repeat the question. Sergeant Virkov was all right, he was fair. He was a good NCO. Fifteen years service. But he was short tempered. He might say that Jrovnic needed to diet, and Jrovnic knew he would not eat for a couple of days. And Sergeant Virkov seemed unusually tense. It was best to leave him alone. We drove on, and I was glad Jrovnic kept quiet.

I didn't like it. Something was up. Why were they sending us ten miles out into the maquis just for some jerk taking tourists hostage? It didn't make sense. And why four snipers? The best marksmen in the regiment. We might be going into a big fight. But Sergeant Virkov knew what he was doing. He had been at Kolwezi. If he needed something else he would have brought it. Still, I was nervous. Not afraid, but nervous. I wanted it to go right, whatever it was, like all those years ago at school before a rugby match. A tension in the pit of the stomach, butterflies they called it. I'd felt the same way before a music exam. I didn't want to let the side down. If I was afraid, it was a fear of messing up in some way that might get someone killed, or at best make us look like fools in front of the gendarmes. That was inexcusable. I glanced at the police car. The two cops never changed their expression. They were dumb clots, the gendarmes, good for nothing other than cracking Arab skulls, looking tough, and fucking dumb women. Normally we were enemies, but here we were, driving together through the stifling heat to something we didn't know. Jrovnic grinned, Thinking? Maybe, I replied, If you could call it that.

The truck began to slow. Clothard and Donnell checked their weapons, even though they knew they were ready. We've arrived, muttered Donnell. The police cars passed us. Jrovnic spat, There they go, the bastards. Now they'll find they didn't need us and we'll have wasted our time, and missed lunch. Let's see, I said, I don't think so, something's up. Stacy stopped. Sergeant Virkov leaned round. OK, out, he ordered, You're all ready. Looking forward to it, said Clothard. Everyone stared because he had spoken. Beyond, at a turn in the road, I could see the gendarmes, four of them, kneeling behind a car. Look at them, said Jrovnic, Young ladies. Shut it, hissed Sergeant Virkov, From now on no-one speaks except me. You say one more thing Jrovnic, you're on a charge. One cop had a megaphone. Pistol in hand, he began to shout the usual, Put down your weapons and surrender, we have you surrounded. I repeat, we have you surrounded, you cannot escape. It sounded ridiculous, like out of a movie. Incoherent screaming beyond the fork in the road, then shouting in accented French, a German by the sound of it. Obscenities. The voice vaguely familiar. But it was a long way off. Sergeant Virkov motioned for us to follow.

We reached the cars. The cop repeated his message. This time the reply was a gunshot, then four more. The slugs slammed into the car. Everyone lay in the dust. The heat seemed to intensify. Burning heat and dust. I tried to swallow. A woman's voice talking over the radio about a traffic jam near the Old Port. This one's for you, said a cop, You get on with it. Sergeant Virkov motioned for me to follow. He crawled to the edge of the car, peered round the bumper and, like a sprinter at the beginning of a race, he knelt briefly before launching himself into the undergrowth. I did the same, slower because I was lugging the rifle. Clothard and Donnell lay at either end of the car, squinting down the rifles. Stacy remained by the truck. Sergeant Virkov whistled, and Jrovnic squirmed through the dirt to the other car abandoned by the cops. The cop with the megaphone spoke again. More incoherent screaming, one of the tourists yelling for mercy, a woman, the sound cut off by a dull thump. More gunshots, bullets shattering the windshield. Whoever it was knew how to shoot. I followed Sergeant Virkov into the trees. He knew exactly where to go. I thought about Kolwezi.

Lying in the fragrant leaves, in the dappled light, we could see the hostages. Above us a bird, shrill, monotonous, repeating hee hee hee hee. An ugly woman lay unconscious by a Renault. Inside, two children sat staring ahead as if they were watching TV. A man sat hunched in the driver's seat, sweating, pale with fear. The father. I saw the gunman kneeling behind the car, no shirt, lean like a cyclist, very fit. His arms tanned, white at the shoulders where he had been wearing short sleeves. A laborer maybe. You've got him, murmured Sergeant Virkov, One shot, he's yours. I leveled the rifle, arranging the sights, squinting into the lens. The view blurred, then came into focus. My heart jumped. Broken nose, scar, he'd shaved his head. It was Mueller. Legionnaire Mueller. It's Mueller, I whispered to Sergeant Virkov. I know, he replied, Take him out. When you get a chance. Don't hesitate.

Mueller. I joined with Mueller. We were in all the trials, basic training, the farm. Out of twenty others, it was just Mueller and me. He was a good man, Mueller. He helped me through some serious shit, I helped him. He never mentioned why he joined. Then again no-one talked. It was part of the tradition. Almost a joke. Mueller. One night, he and I fought some paras, pussy career paras in it for the pension, and then we all fought the police. After he insulted the barman's wife. He was a crazy bastard, he could do fifty pull-ups with his knees at ninety degrees. He never got tired, Sergeant Virkov said he was the best recruit he'd ever seen, and we should all try to be like Mueller. Now Mueller was going to die over some stupid fucking tourists. I wanted to shout, Mueller, it's me, put the gun down. But I knew it was no use. Even if he gave up, he was looking at serious time, and he wasn't the type to do that. He was going to go out the way he wanted. I wondered if he knew who we were. Clothard, Jrovnic, Donnell, Stacy, Sergeant Virkov, we were the same company. But he had deserted. He wasn't one of us any more. One day he wasn't there, a gun was missing, and they were looking for him. We were all interrogated. Why had he gone? How did he get the gun? No-one knew. He just disappeared. That was two months ago. And here he was. He looked the same. I wondered what he had been doing. He'd made few friends, if the tourists were anything to go by. Fucking worthless tourists always getting into trouble. I wondered if the others knew who it was. Sergeant Virkov interrupted my thoughts, What're you waiting for? Shoot.

I observed through the sights. Mueller was leaning against the car, concentrating in the heat. He looked like he hadn't been eating. He was pale. I could see the sweat rolling down his face. His ribs. The corrugated muscles of his stomach. He was carrying a large service pistol, the one he had stolen. The cross hairs split his gaunt face into four neat mathematical sections. Hitherto, I had only fired at a target, sometimes water melons to emulate blood. I knew what an exploding bullet could do. I could hear the cop shouting again over the megaphone like a ritual. Last rites, a prayer. Frowning, Mueller raised the pistol to fire. Momentarily, his head evaded the cross hairs. I adjusted quickly. He was framed again. Now. I squeezed the trigger, feeling the jolt, the brief crack of the discharge like a fire work. I adjusted again, watching, knowing I hit him. A sitting duck. Mueller continued to kneel, the gun in his hand. For a moment, terrified about what Sergeant Virkov would do, I thought I had missed. I could see no wound. Time stopped. Then, with a strange smile, Mueller wheeled about, falling back away from the car. Slow motion. As he turned, I noticed that one side of his cranium was missing, completely gone. Now I saw the result, spattered over the side of the Renault. He slumped into the dust. Through the sights, reality speeding up, the cops raced for a shot, trying to get in on the show. Too late. They knew it was over. A farce. Sergeant Virkov patted me on the back. Nice work, he said, Very clean, well done. He stood up brushing off sand.

Everyone was standing around waiting. A cop was calling for an ambulance. Mueller did not have the dignity of returning to the barracks. He was no longer one of us. He would go to one of the state funeral houses. No-one would claim him. He would be buried in a community grave. Stacy touched my shoulder, handing me a lighted cigarette. I thanked him, smoking it slowly, hoping Jrovnic would leave me alone.

TV Dinner

Steak for supper, a lovely Chateaubriand, I'll cook it rare. And vegetables, broccoli, potatoes, carrots. Steamed. Nothing better. Raining outside. I'll drink my beer. Watch the golf later.

The fatal accident took place outside Sausalito at around 5.20 p.m. just as rush hour traffic was starting to build up. All the victims died of head injuries. Sheriff Johnson said he had never seen anything like it. Looked like a real bad road kill, said the Sheriff.

Hey, honey, do you think you could change the channel? I'm cooking my supper.
Sure honey.
There it goes, vegetables boiling nicely, I'll start the steak. One more sip of beer.

Israeli troops shot dead another five Palestinians today after serious disturbances in downtown Jerusalem. The bodies were riddled with bullets. They were virtually unrecognizable, said family members enraged at the violence.

Hey honey, can you please change to another channel? I'm cooking my supper.
Sure honey, sorry.
See the blood glistening out of the meat. A little fat. I shouldn't. But man, this is going to be good. Love it rare. The rarer the better. Can't wait. Haven't had a good piece of steak like this for so long. Ulcer's better now. No more bleeding.

The Ebola virus is one of the most deadly known to man. Nearly always fatal, the symptoms are particularly disturbing. The victim bleeds massively from all orifices. Violent sneezing rapidly spreads the disease as a halo of mucous and blood sprays the area. One drop of blood in an eye can mean contagion. Contagion means death.

Hey honey, for God's sake can you watch something else? I'm cooking steak. I'm about to eat.
Sorry honey.
There. Ready to serve. At last. Love it when the blood runs onto the plate like that so I can mop it up with the potatoes. Just like I did when I was a kid. No-one ever served it like Mom. Till she had her stroke. July 4th. Eat it rarer if I could.

Victims of the Hiroshima bombing were so badly burned that their skin fell off as they tried to move. Others simply vaporized, their only remains shadows where the intense heat and light literally photographed them onto solid surfaces.

For the love of Christ honey, will you turn that damn thing off? I'm eating. Can't you understand? How can I enjoy my goddamn steak with all that on?
Sorry honey. How's the meat? Hope it's tender. I got it specially from Safeway.

And the champion's backed up in a corner. Lopez is punching. My God this is terrible, what a turnaround. What d'ya think Jim? Well, I've never seen anything like it. And he's coming back. The blood is pouring down his face. I think it's a huge gash above the eye. Blood everywhere. This can't go on. I've never seen a cut so bad.

Hey Sugar. Leave it on, will you? Boxing. D'ya mind if I watch the boxing while I eat my supper?

The Station Master

Speeding across England, my only concern was that I should reach Scotland before the expected blizzard, otherwise my aunt would worry. It was just before World War Two, in the last days of steam. The journey was uneventful, and I dozed in the warm compartment. Roused by the periodic screams of the whistle, I watched the short day ebbing into night, the watery blue twilight fading over the bare English countryside. I felt a twinge of satisfaction, three weeks holiday, Christmas to look forward to, and a feeling that life was going rather well. Cambridge agreed with me, it was certainly better than boarding school. For the first time in my life I had my own room, and plenty of quiet in which to work.

We reached York on time. Then a guard was walking alongside the train, swinging a lantern, shouting, All passengers for Scotland change here. Isn't it going to Edinburgh? I yelled. Nay lad, he replied, Platform two's what you want. Irritated, I lumbered out of the train dragging my luggage, inhaling the freezing air. Squinting in the poor light, I made my way across the vast station. The only other passenger was a rather blousy female. Is this the right platform for the Scotland train? I asked. I wouldn't know deary, she said, I'm only going as far as Catterick.

We waited, neither of us speaking. At last a train arrived. I wandered over to the guard and inquired, Is this the train to Scotland? Tugging at his watch, he grinned, Ay lad, ye take this to Boseby, then ye'll catch the Scotland train in the morning. I was aghast, In the morning? He checked the watch, Ay lad, there's no more tonight, ye'll have to wait till morning. I looked at the clock, And what time does it come through in the morning, in Boseby? Nine, replied the guard, Nine o'clock, ye'll have to take a hotel or something, it's going to be mighty cold.

We reached Boseby at ten. I had no idea where I was, maybe somewhere on the edge of the Moors, a tiny station, beyond a vast expanse of woods. I could hear the wind whistling through the leaves, the creaking of the branches making it seem as if the trees were speaking to one another. Occasionally, the moon emerged from behind low gray clouds scudding in from the west. The first hint of the storm. There was no sign of a hotel. Not that I had money for a hotel. I had barely enough for a bottle of beer. I looked at my watch. Eleven hours. At least there was an end in sight, even if it was eleven hours away.

I found that I was dozing, despite flurries of snow that twirled and whispered to the ground from the angry sky. Twelve o'clock. It was too cold to sleep. I stood up, flapping my arms, stamping my feet. Nine more hours. Something caught my eye, a lamp moving beyond the signals. The station master on his nightly rounds. Through the snow, I saw an old man with a long white beard, impeccably dressed in a uniform, his watch chain shining. Good evening, I said, Cold night to be about. The old man stopped and stared, That it is lad, that it is, and what would ye be doing here this late, if I might ask? Waiting for the Scotland train that's due in at nine, I explained. He frowned, Ah, the Scotland train, ye've a long wait, thy'll be catching your death out here if you don't get in. Is there a hotel nearby? I ventured. He scratched his head, Only thing like that round here is the Eight Bells Inn in Metherby, and that's four miles away, I think you're in a bit of a fix. Well, I mused, It's only another eight or so hours. He pondered the situation before continuing, Tell ye what, just this once, I'll let you into the station house there and you can rest some, and get out of the cold. How does that sound? Are you sure? I asked, I mean, I don't want to cause any inconvenience. He smiled, Nay lad, don't worry, it be right as rain as far as I'm concerned, and anyway, I'm the station master, come on.

We walked along the platform to a small waiting room. He pulled out a wad of keys, Ye'll do better inside, there ye go. I can't tell you how grateful I am, I said, It really was getting rather cold. Think nothing of it, he insisted, I can see you're a good lad, ye remind me of me own, me only dear son, what was killed in t' Great War. The Somme, 1916. Ye get on now, get some rest, Scotland train'll be here in t' morning. He began to wander away. Thank you again, I called. He turned and waved and disappeared into the night. I settled down in the shelter, pulled a scarf over my head, and promptly fell asleep.

Someone was shaking me. Bleary, I turned over, thinking I was still in my rooms at Cambridge and I mumbled, What on earth do you want? Then I snapped awake. I was looking into the face of an angry young man, uncannily similar to me, dressed in the uniform of a station master. It was starting to become light. Aham, I am sorry, I apologized sitting up, I must have been dreaming, by the way, what time is it? I'll say so, said the man, And I'd like to know who you are and what you're doing and how you got into the building. And don't be asking me the time, I've a mind to call the constable, we'll be having no tramps here you know. My good sir, I replied, Despite the appearance of my greatcoat, I am no tramp, merely a traveler waiting for the Scotland train, waiting since ten last night I might add, and I'm heartily sick of the whole thing. Ye still haven't told me how you got in, persisted the young man, This place is locked at night, no-one allowed. I stood up, attempting to appear respectable, The station master let me in, because it was so cold, if you really must know. The station master? quizzed the man, The station master? I am the station master. Then you must be the junior station master, I countered, The man who let me in was quite old, in fact he was very old, he had a long white beard. The young man went pale, A long white beard you say? Exactly, I continued, A long white beard, now if you'll kindly tell me whether the Scotland train is on time and where I should go to catch it because I am thoroughly sick of this journey, and I just want to reach my destination. Clearly upset, the man ignored my question, Ye don't know what you're saying, ye've just described my father, the old station master, he died three years back, and I've been station master since. Ye saw my father, you did. How can ye know?

Briefly, I reached round for my suitcase. Now listen here, I said turning, but the man had vanished. Looking about, wondering where he had gone, thinking I was losing my mind, I stumbled outside. A train was approaching. I waved frantically. Scrutinized by curious passengers, I scrambled aboard. Shaking with fear, I breathlessly asked a businessman where the train was going. Where d'you think? Edinburgh, of course, he replied as if I were a madman. I peered around, expecting to emerge from a bizarre dream. But the train shunted off, and I glanced at my watch. It was nine o'clock precisely.

Years later after the war, another world, another era, I was on a motoring holiday with my wife. We found ourselves near the village of Boseby, and I insisted we visit. It's very lovely, I explained. After driving through the tiny hamlet, with the station and the woods beyond, we ate lunch at the Eight Bells Inn in Metherby. We were the only ones in the pub, and I started a conversation with the publican. Eventually, after a couple of pints, I described the circumstances I have related, the first time I had told anyone for fear of being institutionalized. Far from being incredulous, the publican laughed and said, Ye saw Old George and his son Arthur. Very sad about the boy, killed on the Somme he was like so many lads from the area. Always wanted to be station master like his father. People encounter them now and then. They're always there to help. Who's the present station master? I inquired. The publican grinned, That'd be Jonas Flimby, and very much alive he is, aren't you Jonas? That's him over in the corner. I looked, but I saw no-one.

Trapped Monkeys

Under Lord Milford, we'd controlled the natives by alternately suppressing and encouraging civil strife, playing the tribes off against each other. For years we maintained a stability of sorts. But a leader had appeared, now they were uniting against us. The rebels everywhere, yet they were nowhere. We'd sort things out in one area trying to hang onto the jewel, and they'd pop up somewhere else. All of us claiming God, assuring each other of our right to be, assuring each other of the opposition's guaranteed destruction. The liberals reminding us of our moral role, forgetting that they had the luxury of being liberal because the barbarians were not yet breaking down the gates. The Colonial Office made it very clear there was nothing they could do, if things went wrong we were on our own. If we relinquished the colony, everyone would know the Lion was losing its teeth. We had the means to win, of course, within a short time, but it would make us more savage than the savages we were fighting. Ultimately, it would come to this. Lord Milford knew, and he completely caved in. The poor fellow wasted away. Now I was in charge until a replacement could be found, but candidates were not forthcoming.

I hadn't slept properly in months. My old friend Brigadier Caruthers insisted I take some time off, You're going to end up like Lord Milly, old chap, he joked trying to make the best of it. He knew how bad things were, he'd been proposing we get out, hand the whole mess over to the natives. It's what they bloody well deserve, he postulated, After all we've done for them, let's leave it to them and see where they get to, bloody monkeys the lot of them. I repeated for the umpteenth time how it wasn't that simple, but I knew he wasn't convinced, I knew he was right, although I was loathe to admit it to myself. I had to maintain appearances. He smiled, It's time you got away from it all, just for a few days, give yourself a proper break old chap, spot of hunting in the Highlands, what, that'll put you right. Aside from the heat it was almost like

Scotland up there, excellent trout steams too. Good old Caruthers. We served in the Black Watch. Now he was Director of Mines.

Thus it was, somehow I found myself drenched in sweat ensconced in ferns, a tick burrowing into my neck. I wondered what the hell I was doing, what Caruthers was up to, why we couldn't just use the rifle. But he'd insisted, he wanted to prove something, he'd used the word didactic. A small sum of money hinging on the result. Caruthers covered in leaves. We'd been in the undergrowth for quite some time. The troop above us, chattering in the branches, the crude bamboo cage an attraction. The worst that could happen was a leopard might roam into the vicinity, scaring them away.

The monkey squatted at the edge of the trees. A large male Wadell's Grey. He ambled into the clearing, a couple of others beyond. Caruthers was shaking with suppressed laughter, barely able to control himself. Eyes twitching, the monkey studied the cage. He reached out touching briefly, retreating for renewed contemplation. He approached again, the plantain within too much to resist. Very slowly he leaned in, seizing the fruit. He backed away with the prize, finding he was unable to proceed because his fist would not pass through the bars. Caruthers had attached the contraption to a tree. The monkey pulled to no avail. He waited. Then he tried again. No luck. He discarded the plantain, withdrawing his hand, circling the cage, pushing at it. Then he quickly grabbed the plantain once more. Watch, muttered Caruthers. He rose, releasing the safety catch on the Webley. The troop became silent. The monkey jumped, screeching, baring his teeth, but he would not abandon the object.

Wiping sweat from my eyes, I touched the bump on my neck. The monkey stared, his emerald eyes blinking. Caruthers aimed, squeezing the trigger. The creature's head disappeared in the explosion, the body somersaulting. Above us, the monkeys fled to the forest screaming. Caruthers replaced the pistol in the holster. He lit a cigarette, handing me the water bottle, Told you so old chap, I told you so, learned it from a fakir in India, minus the gun of course. He frowned, By the way old man, you've got a tick in your neck. Yes, I said. He held the cigarette towards my throat. I felt the heat, the insect struggling to escape. Caruthers found his penknife, extracting tweezers, There. He displayed the creature, legs moving black with blood beneath the flat body. Valet, he added, positioning it above the cigarette. The tick popped, disappearing in a thread of smoke.

Thanks, I muttered, picking up the rifle, spots before my eyes. The monkey twitched, a leg kicking. I'd read about the trick, but I'd never seen it performed. Caruthers chuckled, You wait till we cook the bugger, delicious, monkey soup. I smiled, Yes, and I owe you ten Guineas. Caruthers lifted the carcass by the tail, When he'd shown me, when he had the beast by the scruff, the fakir said to me, See yourself here Sahib, learn and you might be wise. Like looking down one of your mine shafts, I said. Caruthers nodded, the last rays of sunlight catching his green eyes, Just a matter of time. Why I brought you here, old man, I knew you'd understand. We trudged to the tent in silence. Glenlivet, Caruthers announced, pouring from the flask, A case arrived a week ago. Sipping the whisky, wondering if I would ever see Scotland again, I built the fire while Caruthers skinned the monkey.

The Prayer Book

Three years after it was all over, Armstrong's mother called. She said something very odd happened, she had received a package from Buenos Aires, via Cambridge. Inside was Armstrong's prayer book. There was a letter in Spanish. She wanted to meet. I readily agreed. I remembered his final night, the night of the patrol.

The rain lashing the dugout. Mid-May, it had been raining for a week. We were waiting for it to become dark, then we were going out. Armstrong's first time across the lines. We knew the Argies had reinforcements, quite naturally we wanted to have a look. Armstrong was reading his prayer book. Saying your prayers again? I asked. Armstrong looked up and smiled. We all laughed. Won't do you any good here, grumbled Caruthers quietly.

Twenty years old, just out of Sandhurst, Armstrong arrived two days before. He was a pretty fellow, fair skinned, with long dark eyelashes. I don't think he was even shaving regularly. God knows what he was doing in the Falklands. It was the thing to do supposedly, in his family, father, grandfather, great-grandfather, career military. Scots Guards. I rather liked him. He was quiet, and very well-read. Apparently, he had the option of going to Oxford.

Ignore him, I said, Here, have some of this, you can only get this in Caithness. I handed him a flask of MacPhail's. Armstrong smiled, blushing like a girl. He swallowed a little, coughing slightly. Thanks, he said, returning the flask. I drank deeply, the whisky warming my chest. I didn't want to become too attached, it was inadvisable. The first couple of engagements were the test. Caruthers and I had served in Ireland and Belize, we'd seen action here, so to some extent we knew what it was about.

It saved my father's life, you know, said Armstrong suddenly, That's why, look. Caruthers grinned, How about his soul? Shut it, I hissed, Leave him alone. I examined the book. A hole neatly drilled through the worn leather, turning left into the thick pages. A bullet, said Armstrong, At El Alemain. He had it in his left shirt pocket. Saved his life. Amazing, I said. Remarkable thing is,

Armstrong continued, He later met the German who shot him. How? I asked. Armstrong leaned against the dugout wall, We were on holiday in Mallorca. I was about seven, my brother was nine. There was a German family. We got to know their two sons, and one night we had dinner together. It was early spring, and there weren't many tourists. The two men started talking about the war. It turned out they had both fought in North Africa. We all knew the story of how my father was in a sandstorm trying to navigate from the turret of the tank, it was the only thing we knew about him from the war because he didn't really talk. Couldn't see a thing, then out of the blue a German tank appeared, the German was doing the same thing, saw my father and shot him, but the prayer book saved his life. The bullet knocked him unconscious but no real damage. We still have the bullet, it was from a Lugar. Anyway, they went on talking exchanging stories, and it turned out they'd been in the same sector, same dates, same time even. It was extraordinary. Then the German became very serious. I will never forget, he said in his heavy accent, We were trying to find our way through this terrible sandstorm, we were lost, completely lost. And suddenly out of the storm there is a British tank, an officer in the turret, right in front of us. So I shot him. I saw him fall back into the tank. It has haunted me ever since, I still dream of it. My God, said my father quietly, That was me. He showed the German the prayer book, he never went anywhere without it, and the two became lifelong friends. They used to go fly-fishing in Bavaria every year until my father died a couple of years ago. Herr Kruger came to his funeral. We still keep in touch with the family. Caruthers lit a cigarette, inhaling deeply, An amazing story. Remarkable indeed, I agreed. Armstrong smiled.

We departed at 3.00 a.m. We found out what we needed but we lost Armstrong, shot through the head as we were trying to get back to our lines. Later, we retrieved the body. Half his head was missing, the prayer book was gone. Bloody thieving bastards, said Caruthers, Fat lot of good his prayer book did him. I didn't reply. We took Port Stanley in the summer, came home heroes, within a year or so everyone had forgotten the war. I met Mrs. Armstrong at the memorial service, told her about her son, how he died instantly. He received a posthumous decoration.

We sat in the living room of the old country house. November, the rain coming down in sheets. I sipped the whisky. MacPhail's by strange coincidence. Mrs. Armstrong handed me the prayer book. It was virtually unrecognizable. The leather had rotted, the pages stuck together, black with blood. Quite remarkable how these things happen, she said, It was forwarded from Magdalene College. Somehow this has helped me. She handed me the letter. One of his schoolmasters had translated it. I stared at the blue ink, the labored Spanish.

> Dear Mr. Armstrong,
>
> I return this book to you. This book was in the pocket of my son when he was killed in the Battle of Tumbledown Mountain in Las Malvinas. It was returned to me with his belongings. I saw an address and the name of a man, so it should be yours. I know that it brought my son strength in his final days. Maybe you were a soldier or a father. I wish you well though my heart is breaking.
>
> Maria Sanchez

I wrote to her, whispered Mrs. Armstrong fighting back tears, John's Spanish teacher helped me compose the letter, I told her what happened, I'm going to visit her next month, she lives in a suburb of Buenos Aires, you're welcome to come. That is a very wonderful thing, I murmured. I sipped the whisky, contemplating the battered book. In the cover, barely legible: October, 1938. James Armstrong. Magdalene College, Cambridge. A small coat of arms, and a motto: Garde Ta Foy.

Year Abroad

Hey, he said one afternoon, Hey. I ignored him but it was no use. I sat up. Gaz standing unshaven, a candidate for the asylum. What? I mumbled. He cleared his throat, I've just been with them, they're wondering what's wrong with you. He licked his lips, Why you're ignoring them. Walking through the town this morning. Or was it yesterday? The town, a hundred inhabitants, a hotel, a dirt road, one bar, two restaurants, some tarmac they call an airport. Ghost people shuffling through the dust. They were white, British, an embarrassment. Cathy, Rat, Leo, Sarah.

Cathy saw me but she didn't wave, as if she wasn't sure. It was inevitable. We'd meet in the bar, the conversation about soccer, who beat who, the news back home, whether Labour had a chance, who was on strike, British this, British that. Britain the center of it all. I'd get sucked into their rain cloud. The last thing I wanted was a Mancunian talking about soccer. Or Leo's socialism. And Cathy had ditched me. Why I'd come here in the first place. I didn't understand. In a country this big, they, and especially she, had to come to the precise place where I had found some peace. I couldn't be fucked, that's all, I replied, Am I under some obligation? He waited. Do you want to swim? I asked. No, Cathy wants to see you, he muttered. I blew my nose into the sand, blocking one nostril, then the other, Tell her I'll meet her here, tell her to come in about an hour.

He loped towards the jungle, back to the hut. I stood up and stretched. The turquoise ocean, the sun setting fire to shreds of purple cloud on the horizon. The waves picked up like glass, standing momentarily, shattering onto the surface. I waded, ducking under the walls of whitewater. I caught wave after wave, my hand slicing into the crests, riding four foot toboggans of foam. After a long time, I remembered. Rising and falling on the swell I could see the beach far away. Someone sitting. It was her. I waited, wondering how long she would stay. She didn't move so I took a wave, the water embracing me, hurling me onto the sand. I picked myself up and marched towards her. Standing at attention, I saluted shouting, Corporal Rawlings reporting for duty, sah.

She was smoking, gently tapping the ash into the breeze. Very pretty. She pushed a strand of dark hair out of her cat green eyes, Don't be so stupid. Why did you ignore me? I sat down, Oh, I just didn't want to see you, that's all, not you I mean, I added hastily, I mean the others. She stared, It wasn't very nice you know. What do you expect? I countered, trying to be cold, After everything, why did you come? I'm going home, she murmured, I had to see you. She leaned back, shutting her eyes, drawing aimlessly in the sand, I'm going to fly out tomorrow. You're going? She motioned vaguely, Yeah. Got a cig? She offered me a crumpled packet, Does it matter? I took one and lit it, inhaling deeply. I flicked the ash away, What about the university authorities? Fuck them, she scowled, If they don't like it they can go to hell. I shouldn't have to stay here if I don't want to. And who cares as long as I get my thesis done?

We smoked the cigarettes, watching the sun's rays sinking into the vastness. What happened? She stubbed out her cigarette, throwing the filter away, You left. And something happened with me. My heart jolted, When? She inhaled quickly, Oh, nothing. Nothing, but it could have, it was close, it scared me. I persisted, When? She became agitated, Oh, one night, a few days after you left, when we'd gone to a bar. A guy thought I'd given him signals, he actually suggested screwing me up the back entrance so my supposed virginity would remain intact, can you believe? God, I muttered. But Rat was there and it was all sorted out. Rat? Yeah, Rat. Always Rat, I yelled, the skinny lad with John Lennon glasses, knowing he'd fucked her, wondering how he did it, the reason I left, Always Rat, is that why you came here, to tell me that? Please, she whispered, I'm so sorry, I'm so very sorry, please don't. She touched my hair, I need to talk to you, there were a couple of things, please let me tell you, I've got to talk to you, please. I stared at her. She tried to smile, glancing away. On the way here. We were coming from Veracruz on the bus. Hours and hours. I have no idea.

240 miles on the map. What is it about this place? Time and distance don't make sense anymore. Twenty four hours to get to Oaxaca alone. I don't understand, I don't even know how long it took in the end, the journey seemed to go on and on. I had to sit next to this old man. He was very sweet. We're traveling up these slopes, in a school bus, up mountains, the road was as wide as a double bed. I saw the wrecks of buses down in the canyons. Anyway, there we are, mile after mile, hour after hour, and I fall asleep. I wake up, and the old man is snuggling up to me. I think, OK mate, that's enough of that. I look down and he's got a hard on. Sticking up in his trousers, like a handle. It's obvious. I try to push him back but he moves closer. And he's rigid, you know, rigid. I thought he was messing around. Then I feel his skin, by chance, his arm brushes my hand. Stone cold. And suddenly I realize, he's dead. Dead. I'd never seen a dead person before. I screamed. They stopped the bus, but there was nothing anyone could do. What can you do after all? He was dead and they had to go on. And no-one seemed bothered, no-one reacted, even the others, that's what really did it. They were more surprised that I'd screamed. Night was falling and the driver wanted to be out of the sierra as soon as possible. I thought we were all going to die. So I traveled with the dead man leaning up against me for the next I don't know how many fucking hours. I had enough, that was it for me. My God, I whispered, stroking her hair.

The darkness came quickly, stars spattering the sky. I lit a cigarette and gave it to her, lighting one for myself. She looked at me, panicked, There was something else, here, on this beach. The first day, before you knew we'd arrived, we walked on the beach in the dawn before sleeping. Twenty four hours in the bus, maybe more, half of that with the dead man, and I get here and I can't sleep. So Rat and I walk on the beach. Hey, look, I interrupted, I don't need to hear this. Can you shut the fuck up about Rat? Her eyes filled with tears, It's over, it was nothing, Rat, he's nothing, he's useless, it's why I came all this way to see you, please understand, please, what did you expect the way you were behaving then? It wasn't just me, I inhaled holding the smoke in my lungs, exhaling slowly, It takes two to tango. Alright, you were saying, you saw something. She cleared her throat wiping her face, Yes, I saw something washed up. We went to look, thinking it was a dog or a seal or something. It was a body, a young man, half a young man. Just a rib cage, a pelvis and some flesh, the crabs were eating him, I threw up. Christ, I muttered, The West German who drowned, the sharks must have been at him. He disappeared the other day. You found him? Did you report it? Yes, she said, We did, we went to the police. I've had enough, I want to get out. Twice it's happened. I don't want a third, and I know it's going to happen if I stay. Something terrible. This place is bad, I want to leave. I hate it.

I hugged her, smelling the floral scent of her hair, knowing I loved her despite everything. That's why I came, she whispered, I wanted to talk to you, I love you. I knew you'd understand. I wanted to see you, you're the only one I could talk to. Nothing's the same anymore. The others were strange too, they don't really want me around, they think I'll bring them bad luck. I mean English university students, can you believe it? They're starting to behave like a bunch of savages. They think I'm jinxed. Sarah said I was a Jonah. In two days I'll be in Heathrow. Can you believe it? Heathrow. She began to laugh. It'll all be over, she added, Like a bad dream. I could hear the surf, the ocean glittering with starlight. The breeze brushed us like a heavy wet towel, pungent with the dank odor of vegetation.

She fidgeted, I'd better be going. I just want to sleep, I can't do anything else. I haven't slept in days. I suppose so, I said, You could stay with me in the hut if that idiot Gaz wasn't there, but that's the way it is. Come on then. I pulled her up. We walked hand in hand through the jungle to the road. The night alive with heat and insects. She smiled, Well, I'll see you, I'd invite you in but I've just got to sleep. I stroked her hair, That's OK, don't even think about it. I leaned towards her and kissed her. Our tongues touched. I wanted to tell her I loved her. She ruffled my hair, I'll see you back in Blighty. I started singing, We'll meet again, don't know where, don't know when, only know we'll meet again some sunny day. She waved. I watched her walking up the dirt road to the hotel, a ramshackle place with a rotting verandah. She looked back and I blew a kiss. I love you, I muttered. The small vulnerable figure disappeared. I'd see her in the autumn, I'd tell her then. I'd ask her to marry me. Depressed, tears in my eyes, I ambled towards the beach. I lay on the sand, staring at the stars, the surf lulling me to sleep.

I returned to Britain just in time for October registration. Thatcher had been voted back. The country drabber than ever, unemployment at an all time high, and I wondered how the British put up with it year after year, let alone why. You get used to anything. I had the winter to look forward to, and a schedule I left behind a year and a half before. The middle class illusion of university life, the red brick wall. I'd received a card from Cathy posted in Mexico City months before. She signed it I love you. I strolled towards the faculty to register, nervous to meet her, swirling leaves, rain pelting the dirty old city. A storm had moved across the Atlantic, full of warm air. I watched it developing on the weather report after the six o'clock news. The warm rain fell on my face, I thought about how it came from Mexico. I had a beard, and I was so tanned people thought I was an immigrant.

I searched for her. This time we'd keep it going. She would help me, I'd be there for her. I couldn't wait to see her smile, hear her laugh, her sense of humor, she'd put it right. We'd go for a beer, I'd put my arm around her, run my hand through her hair, we'd never stop talking, I'd tell her how much I missed her, I'd tell her I loved her. We'd make love. Hello Dr. Wright, I said, seeing my tutor. I didn't recognize you Andy, he replied, Do you have a moment? Back in body perhaps, the mind is otherwise occupied, I drawled trying to be clever. Have you seen Cathy at all? Come with me for a moment, he mumbled.

He drew me aside, shutting the door of his office, his arm around me. He stared, his eyes too moist. She's dead Andy, he murmured. Dead? The word like a bullet. Dead? Dead? How can she be dead?

She's dead, he repeated, She was killed in a car crash in Mexico City a few months ago, on the way to the airport. She was coming home, apparently she wasn't feeling well. I'm, I mean, we're very sorry, terribly sorry, it's really dreadful, she was a lovely girl, beautiful, she was very able as you know. She had great potential. We're having a memorial for her, next week, when the term's started, when everyone's settled, it's so very very sad. I was starting to break down, and I didn't want him to see me crying. I'm going, I whispered. Then I was sobbing. Dr. Wright nodded, I quite understand, I'm terribly sorry. I walked down the corridor and stepped outside, the Mexican rain mingling with my tears.

The Flying Doctors

Dr. Rees, I presume, said Caruthers looking through the binoculars, He's late. Must be the storm. Wiping the sweat from my eyes, I stared into the shimmering distance from the shade of the acacia, Let's hope it breaks soon, relieve us of the heat. Indeed, Caruthers agreed, Stifling. He waved at the boys spread across the hillside, Daktari Rees. They waved back, they would be there till dusk. We were catching tsetse flies, to find the rates of sleeping sickness in the area. Against all trends, an epidemic of Trypanosoma brucei rhodesiense had developed in the last few months, and Tom Rees was going to provide inoculations of pentamidine to some Maasai exhibiting early symptoms.

Against the billowing thunderclouds, the tiny speck grew larger. Then I heard the engine. The little plane wobbled in the updrafts, beginning its descent. Below us, Maasai congregated near the trees. The Cessna circled, turning into the wind, before landing on the dirt strip. The pilot taxied towards the village, coming to a halt. The Maasai ran towards the plane, surrounding the two men as they climbed down the ladder. That's Tom, said Caruthers, You can spot him a mile off with that shock of fair hair. Come on, let's say hello. We wandered down the hill. He won't be away till tomorrow afternoon at the earliest, that's for sure, Caruthers continued, If it really rains could be a good deal more, haven't seen him for nearly a year, absolute wonders what he and those other fellows have done for the region. I nodded, McIndoe did miracles too for a Dakota pilot I knew, caught in a burning plane, you know. Caruthers raised an eyebrow, That fellow Edwards you mentioned, isn't he acting now? I nodded, Jimmy Edwards, yes, incredible, one would never know. Arnhem, Caruthers muttered, Seems so long ago. We rolled the blue net of tsetse, and I placed it in the basket, Give us some idea at least, when we get the results from Nairobi. Blighters, Caruthers said, Never seems to be anything we can do.

Caruthers extracted a pack of Turkish cigarettes from his bush jacket, lighting one, It may be apocryphal, but Tom once mentioned how he got the idea for this whole lark. He knew this chap George Sayer, a Classics don, a remarkable man actually, really at the top of his game. He was acquainted with people like C.S. Lewis and Tolkien. He was British, his father had been a district commissioner in Nyasaland, but his mother was American. Then he inherited some money, and he decided on a complete change. Oh, he kept his hand in with translation work and the occasional lecture, and he published a couple of text books, but he was free to roam. He loved Africa and he knew how to fly, Tiger Moths mainly, and he had a Cessna he chartered. He'd flown Lysanders for SOE, so he was damn good. He was with three people when the Cessna ran into trouble, he was forced to land in a remote part of Katanga during a rebellion. They were captured by a Luba strongman, and things didn't look too good, the chief couldn't make up his mind whether to kill them or ransom them. But the chief's youngest son fell sick. Of course the natives had overheard Sayer being addressed as doctor. They put two and two together, and the next thing he knew, Sayer had a gun to his head, the chief's son before him, and if he didn't cure the lad it was curtains for all of them. Well, Sayer calculated the boy was suffering because he'd eaten too many grapes. He made a great show, prancing about muttering Latin incantations, making signs above the groaning body, and he forced the patient to drink rancid coffee. The lad proceeded to vomit the grapes, sleeping for several hours, and he awoke completely cured. Well that was that, Sayer had big power, and the tribe were so terrified of him that, based on his demands, he and his colleagues were escorted to safety and handed over to the Belgians.

Caruthers lit my cigarette. Good Lord, I said, exhaling smoke. Quite a tale, Caruthers agreed. What's Sayer doing now? I asked. Not sure old chap, not sure, Caruthers replied, I'm sure Tom knows. By the way, I don't like the look of that storm, it's on its merry way towards us. Let's call it a day, and we'll have some Glenlivet, a case arrived last week, I'll bet Tom will be keen for a dram. He waved his arms yelling, Kiswane m'badele, umpala indebana, inswana Daktari Rees. The nearest boys waved back. They rolled the nets, yelling at the others, and they began to descend the hill. In the distance the sky was turning ink black, the wind rising, and I was glad we were near the village.

Compart Mentis

The rains were late, the sauna heat building upon itself day after day. I sat in the leather armchair drenched in sweat, reading the Port Campbell Times, sipping pink gin. Caruthers was writing a letter to his sister. As usual, the day being Saturday, we were playing a leisurely game of chess. I see the docks have reopened, I observed, referring to a melee involving the crews of two ships that had impeded business for a couple of days. Yes, said Caruthers, At last. Something of a metaphor too, the whole blasted show. Each crew from a different tribe, I added. Caruthers nodded, Exactly what I mean, old chap, the history of civilizations in a nutshell. A dangerous precedent, we can't let that sort of thing happen again, someone might get ideas. Nothing London can do if things go wrong. A major I knew in the Black Watch once said the whole of Scottish history was one long barroom brawl, I saw it reenacted every night in Glasgow, but it applies across the board. I moved my rook, Check. He grinned, Damn you Brodrick, let me think about this one. Furthermore, he continued, It is ironic that the recent problems concerned ships. Why? I asked. He moved his king, Think about it Brodrick.

Failing to understand his analysis, pretending to read the newspaper, I pondered the situation. He had escaped, I'd missed something. His queen still dominated the central squares. I moved my knight, groping for a new attack. A ship sailing on the unpredictable seas is no different from an empire, he resumed, Indeed, it is these very ships, the maritime lifeline, that ensure Britannia continues to rule the waves. Captain at the bridge, sturdy structure, yet no matter how good the crew, only certain vessels will survive a leak. Watertight compartments, I said. He moved a pawn, pinning my queen, Precisely, old chap, precisely, something you missed in this game, I'm afraid.

For a long time I contemplated. Mate in three, I said finally, toppling my king. Afraid so, old man, just a matter of time, makes up for last week. Where are we now? I asked. Not sure, but it's close, I'd have to calculate. Another gin and Angostura? Absolutely, I agreed. He signaled to the bar. Titanic, I said, It was the linking compartments. Yes, Caruthers shouted, Yet we seem not to have learned. Proudest ship of her time, supposedly unsinkable, symbol of everything we are. Uncanny the parallels. Change is coming, I'm afraid, we'll all go down. I had a great-uncle in the Indian Mutiny. Thereafter, as Lord Elphinstone concluded, it was divide the hull into watertight compartments, be it the army, the mines, society. Strong authority, lots of divisions. Don't let them fight each other, and above all don't let them unite against you. The secret of empire, it worked all over the place.

And this Gandhi fellow? I asked. Caruthers stared, Far more dangerous old chap, Lord Louis will be the last Viceroy, I hear water sloshing below the decks. We won't be able to stay, you know. I've thought about it, I muttered, I can't exactly see myself settling in England. What is there after all? Damp cold in Bournemouth, a Labour government, and rationing. Ram arrived with two pink gins. Thank you Ram, I said. It is my very great pleasure, Sahib, he replied shaking his head. Yes, thank you Ram, said Caruthers. You're absolutely right, Brodrick, aside from the fishing, there really is nothing to go back to. However, there is South Africa. Good fishing there, I agreed, I've heard the Drakensberg range is excellent. Climate too, Natal just like here. We can take any of the wallahs that might wish to accompany us. Caruthers laughed, Should provide refuge, for a while at least, worst comes to the worst there's always the estate in Scotland.

Under New Management

Mohammed slept in the dim light of the carriage, his head slumped sideways, broken nose bent double, sunken cheeks so deep his face seemed to be carved from wood. Stained black from tobacco, his lower lip jutted out creating the aura of a hungry animal. His hair tightly curled, short, greasy. I finished the remains of the cigarette, grinding the paper into the wooden slats.

The landscape flickered verdant, countryside gradually surrendering to squat dusty one-road towns, children waving and yelling, running alongside the carriages. Eventually the adobe suburbs of Algiers. The train halted in a siding below a rusting iron bridge. Mohammed rubbed his eyes. Searching for a cigarette, he coughed and spat through the vent. We waited for a goods train to start across the vast distance to the desert settlements, Laghouat, Ghardaia, Ouargla, Timimoun, the wagons clanging by for several minutes. Far away, echoing music over the buildings. Algiers gleaming white, shadows still long, the breeze off the sea fresh and clean.

We jumped from the train into the church cool of the red brick station. Mohammed stripped off his denim jacket and several layers of shirts by a tap, proceeding to swill water over himself. Ah that is good, he mumbled. He patted himself with newspaper, grinning, his stomach corrugated with strength. He stuck a cigarette in his mouth as he dried, puffing merrily, Eh, André, your turn. I splashed water across my face.

I retrieved my luggage from the locker, and we lurched into the sunlight. Against the blue of the sky, gulls soared on the thermals above the azure bay, sparkling in the morning sun, tiny lapping waves twinkling in the light. Cars pushed slowly through the crowds, billowing exhaust. The muezzin's call for prayers drifting on the breeze, Allllah hu Akkkbarr . . . Mohhhhmad Rassssoul . . . LLLa Illllllah Allllllah . . . hu Akkkkkba . . . sending shivers down my spine. Mohammed stopped to listen. Beautiful, I said. He nodded, The muezzin, yes, it makes me strong to hear. Where? He motioned, The great mosque near Bab El Oued. Alllah hu akkkbarr. Allons y. Nous allons chercher l'hôtel. The hotel is in Bab El Oued. We leave the luggage, then we go into the city. We have to sell today.

We wandered by the station precinct past the railway junction and the docks, the brown army barracks, up the hill along the boulevard by the port. From the center we reached Bab El Oued, walking through cobbled streets that narrowed as we neared the Casbah. Mohammed stalked ahead. We were sweating heavily. He turned to me, pointing, Viens. I show you something.

A vast 19th century red brown cathedral, built near the great mosque so that the bells might drown the muezzin, the stained glass intact. The walls pockmarked with bullet holes from the war, the damage like acne. We entered through the west door. A familiar musty hint of incense, the sounds of a surprisingly large congregation. Midday mass was about to commence. Seeking the altar, the hanging body of Christ, I rested with my bag as my eyes grew accustomed to the gloom.

Through the cloisters, the organ loft, the choir stands, the old sacred regions, in the ghostly half-light, bands of women bustled, jostling noisily through stores selling men's underwear, men's suits, magazines, newspapers, pans, brushes, iron goods for the kitchen, women's apparel. The sound of registers, and loudspeakers announcing bargains, echoing through the nave. The altar a restaurant where families were gorging on chicken and chips. Above them, an advertisement claiming the best lamb in Algiers. Slightly nauseated, I found myself admiring the building's new role. Mohammed waved an arm, Isn't it magnificent? Indeed, I agreed, But the lighting could be improved. Mohammed chuckled, ruffling my hair, Come on. I like you, you surprise me. Let's get going.

Two Tones
Melanie's version

I got to Merida in October, October 15th I think it was. It was all right, a bit strange. I was on my own and I was too busy to think about anything the first few days because I was finding a flat and I was walking all over the place. So I wasn't too homesick although I missed Mum and Dad after they saw me off at the airport. I tried going to lectures in the beginning but it was completely crazy. The students turned up but the lecturers never arrived and we just went from room to room and building to building never getting any lectures. So after a couple of days of that I thought, That's it, and I went to the library to do something for my Extended Essay because I was already worried, but the library was about the size of a single room, and all the books were damaged or stolen. It was so hot. I couldn't believe it. I'd only been to Spain with Mum and Dad and that was pretty hot but it was nothing like this. And the insects. You couldn't have your window open without these horrible things coming in, crickets and moths, moths the size of which you've never seen. I liked it though. It was OK. And the people were sweet. Very small and squat, but friendly enough. I didn't go out at night though. It was too scary. There were no street lamps, and it was so quiet. Anyway, no-one goes out on their own after dark, do they? Well, I was the only one there from my university. The others were in Veracruz and Xalapa in the north, and I think someone was in Mexico City, but I'm not sure. I didn't know them well anyway. I stayed around the town not doing much, or just in my flat which I got through an agency the first day which was lucky. I could cook a bit so I could live cheaply, and there were some great markets. I bought some rugs and jewelry. Then some others arrived from Portsmouth, and they were OK. They smoked a lot of grass and they didn't seem to care much about anything, but they were all right. We went out a couple of times to a restaurant and some of the bars, and it was nice to have some people from England because it was all getting a bit isolated there by myself. But there was no-one I particularly liked although they were OK. Well, there was this party at someone's house out of town. I don't know where it was. We got driven there by this guy I never saw again. He was American and he had a jeep. It was about twenty minutes out of town but the road was bad, and we went slowly because of the narrow road, so it probably wasn't that far. I didn't think about how I was going to get back. I just thought, if the others are there, we'll all go together. We'd been in a bar in town, and I'd had a couple of beers but I was sober. Outside the town it was about as dark as it could get. There were no lights at all for miles, just total dark. The stars were out, and it was beautiful. I've never seen the stars like that before, ever. It was as if someone had sprinkled sugar across black velvet. We were at this little ranch, and everyone was drinking tequila and beer. I don't like spirits so I just had a beer and listened to the music. They had these drums and these guys were going crazy drumming this stuff, and they had Santana on the record player, and other Latin American music. Nothing much happened. People danced a bit, but it wasn't one of those really crazy parties. Some of them were smoking huge joints of grass, and I had one puff but it was too strong, and one puff was enough, I knew right away, so I didn't have any more. Then I was in the garden watching the stars, and some other people were there. The light was very soft and mysterious, and it was a beautiful house. I don't even know whose place it was. It was absolutely in the middle of nowhere. I started to wonder how I was going to get home after a while, so I went back to the house, but I couldn't find any of the people from Portsmouth. Then someone said they'd already gone back. They'd been looking for me but they couldn't find me and they thought I'd already gone or that I wanted to stay. I'd been talking to this bloke in the garden, and he seemed sweet. He was dressed in a tennis shirt and jeans, and he followed me into the house. When he heard what had happened, he offered to drive me into town back to my flat. I agreed because he seemed all right, and we talked a bit more for a while. I had another beer, and we watched the guys on the drums. Then I thought I'd better be getting back as it was getting late so I asked

Juan, that was his name, if he'd take me, and he agreed. We said goodnight to everyone, but they were all pretty stoned or drunk, and they didn't really notice so we just left. It was beautiful out, cool and fragrant, and the stars were incredible. The undergrowth was buzzing with insects and cicadas. He had a sports car, and we got in and started to drive slowly down the road, which was just a dirt track, winding through the undergrowth. We drove and drove, and it seemed like we'd never get to the main road. If there was any such thing as a main road. But I didn't worry. It was warm, but not too warm, and it was a lovely night. I could see the lights of the town in the distance, so I was relaxed. It's really flat around there, unlike the north, and you can see for miles. But then he stopped the car when we were still on the dirt track and he started to talk. I listened for a while. He was talking about his family and friends and how he was lonely because they were all in the north, and how he was here and how he didn't like it. I think he was working while he was studying, but he must've had some money to have a car like that. I thought he was up to the old tricks, so I suggested we get back because it was getting late. But he just went on talking, on and on. And there was nothing I could do. I couldn't exactly get out and walk. Even though I could see the town. Then he put his arm around me, and I tried to pull away, but he said, It's all right, it's because I'm lonely, that's all. I tried to push him off but I couldn't. Then he was kissing my neck and he tried to kiss me on the mouth at the same time as his hand grabbed me between the legs, and he tried to undo my jeans. I managed to push him off and jump out of the car. I ran up the road a bit towards the town but I didn't know where I was going, and then I fell. He was onto me right away, and he rolled me over. He already had his jeans undone, and he tried to undo mine, but I struggled and hit him. Then he hit me in the face, hard, and I screamed, so he hit me again. Then I lay still. It was like I was paralyzed. He pulled off my jeans and my panties, and he was between my legs and then he forced himself into me and raped me. I just lay there taking it. I was crying. I couldn't believe it. There was nothing I could do. At first he really hurt me. But after a while

I didn't seem to feel anything. Afterwards he helped me find my jeans and he was very gentle. He led me back to the car. I think I was in shock. I just sat there crying, and he comforted me as though he was my boyfriend. On the way back, coming round a corner in the town, we hit a car and I hit the dashboard and cut my eyebrow open. There was blood everywhere. He drove me to the hospital and stayed with me while they sewed it up. Then he drove me to my flat. I never saw him again. People said he'd gone to the north. A girl once said she'd rather have a terrible scar on her face than be raped. I've got both. They say the scar will disappear eventually when the eyebrow grows back but I know it won't. It'll always be there.

Juan's version

I hate this place. I came here because they sent me. I had no choice. My father's a lawyer and he wanted me to be one too so I can continue the business with his gangster friends and the gringos in the north with all the stuff that goes on. So they sent me here. Where the heat's like nothing else and the place is full of flat heads, those fucking Indians you see everywhere. Yeah I've got a car and money and I don't need to go to school. But after a while you just want to leave. Up north it's different. I can get to California or Arizona and it's different. No fucking flat heads for a start. And California women. I don't need to say anything more. Those gringos don't know how to fuck and the women are just dying for it. Pure Latin lover. The other night I fucked this bitch real good. I was just doing the usual thing, driving around all day. Saturday. Smoked a little maria, drank some tequila, hung out with my buddies, you know, like any other Saturday, except that it's hot, you know, really hot, like it's never been. And I'm lying in my car thinking about the north and feeling lousy as hell. And someone says there's a party on over at someone's farm in the night, so we kill time, and get a little drunk and a little stoned and try to score with some of those bitch flat head women, but no luck. Evening comes and we drive over. Nothing much going on. Just a whole load of stoned guys on the drums, and the garden. And I drank some more tequila and thought what a fucking bore everything was. It just made me miss the north even more. Then later these gringos show up, about five or six. White, and the girls pretty, you know, I mean sweet and clean and new. No sweat or dirt. But it's hard to get to know them, you know, they're cautious, and they're with these gringo boys, nothing tough but it's hard to get to know them. Like they're from a different planet or something. But there was one. A real beauty, in shorts and a T shirt, and she's well built but not fat, and I just start to drip for her. So I go into the garden. I see she's smoked a little but she's not stoned or drunk. I offer her some but she says she's had some beer already. We're talking in the garden and the night's going by, the cool breeze and the stars up there, and she's talking about the stars and how she can't see them like that back home, where she comes from, England, wherever the fuck that is, New England maybe. I heard there's a state called that. Then she says she's got to go, so we go back inside and her friends have all gone. She starts getting worried but I say, I'll take you home, I've got a car. She looks at me and I can tell right there she wants it and I start to get hot for her. She's mine and I know I'm going to get her. We go to the car, and she's close to me. I can smell her, hot, driving me crazy. I'm thinking, This is it, you're going to score buddy, this is it. And I can hardly walk because I'm so stiff. So I put her in the car and we drive off. I mean if she gets in the car that's it, right? That means she wants it. So I'm driving, and it's dark as hell but I know the road. I can smell her all the time, and I'm about busting out of my jeans. She's just in shorts and that T shirt after all, and I'm thinking about her wet and ready. And I've got to do it otherwise she'll think I'm queer or something and maybe it'll get around that Juan had the chance and he didn't do anything, and people will laugh. They'll say, Hey Juan, cabrón, you're a pendejo, man. You a puto? You know how it is. So I stop the car and talk to her. She tenses a little but she listens and she talks a bit. I'm releasing about how I think this place stinks and how I want to go home to the north. Then when I think she's ready I kiss her, I mean I kissed her neck. She struggles a bit as they all do, but then she lets me kiss her on the mouth. She responds so we just kiss for a bit, and then I can't wait any longer, I'm busting, so I put my hand on her leg, between her legs, and go to get her shorts off. Then the bitch starts to fight me and she tries to escape. The little bitch cocktease. She's out of the car and up the road, and I'm after her. I catch her when she falls down. She struggles a bit but then she stops, and she lets me get her shorts off, and her panties, and I can feel that she's dripping for it, I mean she's wet, wet, really wet as I put my fingers in, and then I'm inside her. I fuck her slowly in the road, and she lets me. She comes and then I fuck her again. Afterwards we lie there for a bit and then I take her home. I guess I was drunk or tired but we hit this car coming out of a street, and I'm yelling at this bastard about the damage to my car and he's yelling at me, then we both notice she's cut above the eye. There's blood everywhere, so I drive her to the hospital where they stitch her up, just like a fighter. And she's quiet and nothing wrong, and I'm thinking, This chick's OK, I might see her again, because she doesn't cry or whine when the needle goes in. Yeah, I think, I might see her again. Then I take her home, and I tell her I'll meet her tomorrow. I couldn't sleep. I jacked off a couple of times thinking about her and then I just had enough. I had to get out, drive north I mean, go home. This place can go to hell. I'm not staying any more, so before dawn I packed up and drove off. I'm never going back, and if my father doesn't like it the sonofabitch can go fuck himself for all I care. What does he know? If he thinks it's so good, why doesn't he go and live there himself? So here I am. Half way there, half way home. And I don't know if I'm going home or not. I think about her but I don't know if I want to see her again. Those gringo bitches are too weird. OK for a fuck, and that's it. But that's all they want after all, isn't it? But she was good. Hot, you know, real hot. But I don't know where I'm going. I'll have to decide pretty soon. Or maybe I'll just drive around for a while. I don't know. I'll have to decide.

Publication History

"Art for Art's Sake, Money for God's Sake," *Pindeldyboz*: December, 2004.

"Dirty War," *Franklin's Grace And Other Stories: Winners Of Ireland's Fish Short Story Prize*: 2002.

"Snuff," *Gold Dust:* Summer, 2008.

"The Monkey House," *3:AM Magazine*: February, 2007.

"Apes," *Babel, The Multilingual, Multicultural Online Journal Of Arts And Ideas*: May, 2005.

"The Governor," *The Taj Mahal Review*: December, 2007.

"Cross Words," *Outsider Ink*: Fall, 2004.

"The Purveyor of Fine Toys and Games," *Illogical Muse*: Fall, 2008.

"The Toy Shop," *The Oracular Tree*: January, 2005.

"The Big Man," *The Copperfield Review*: May, 2003.

"Up the River," *971 Menu*: April, 2008.

"The Cutter," *The Duct Tape Press*: February, 2001.

"Teams," *The Oracular Tree*: January, 2005.

"The Game," *The Oracular Tree*: June, 2004.

"The Garden of Remembrance," *Children, Churches And Daddies Literary Magazine*: July, 2005.

"The Links," *The Copperfield Review*: April, 2006.

"Ambush," *The Pedestal Magazine*: June, 2006.

"The Jungle," *Bookpress, The Newspaper Of The Literary Arts*: December, 2001.

"Lions," *EWG Presents*: April, 2003.

"The Last Supper," *Parting Gifts*: 2002.

"Seek and Ye Shall Find," *The Copperfield Review*: April, 2006.

"The Politician," *The Duct Tape Press*: May, 2000.

"The Reunion," *Thought Magazine*: Summer, 2003.

"Sunday Breakfast," *The Duct Tape Press*: May, 2000.

"Sniper," *12-Gauge.Com*: March, 2002.

"TV Dinner," *Urban Graffiti*: September, 2002.

"The Station Master," *EWG Presents*: February, 2003.

"Trapped Monkeys," *The Copperfield Review*: Fall, 2007.

"The Prayer Book," *The Oracular Tree*: October, 2004.

"Year Abroad," *Illogical Muse*: June, 2009.

"The Flying Doctors," *The Istanbul Literary Review*: May, 2009.

"Compart Mentis," *The Copperfield Review*: July, 2009.

"Under New Management," *3:AM Magazine*: February, 2009.

"Two Tones," *The Duct Tape Press*: May, 2000.

About the author

Born in Johannesburg, South Africa, Andrew McIntyre was educated in England, Scotland, Japan, and the United States. He holds master's degrees in Economics and Comparative Literature. He is a member of Magdalene College, Cambridge. He lives in San Francisco.

Andrew's website is www.mcintyre-art.com

Merilang Press Books

www.merilang.com/merilang-press/

You may be interested in other books from Merilang Press:

Books for Adults

Sun on the Hill
Poems from Wales by Daffni Percival

Letters from My Mill
by Alphonse Daudet, translated by Daffni Percival

The Other End of the Rainbow
Short stories by David Gardiner

The Rainbow Man and Other Stories
by David Gardiner

Solid Gold
An anthology of the best prose from 5 years of *Gold Dust* magazine, edited by David Gardiner

Children's Books by Daffni Percival

And Thereby Hangs a Tail
Memoirs of a border collie puppy as he grows up and learns to be a 'good sheepdog' as his mother told him
1st edition (colour), 2nd edition (black & white)

A Sheepdoggerel Anthology
A collection of animal poems with a preponderance of collies

The Rainbow Pony
A bedtime story for young children – small card book